“Would you consid camp cook job for t

In spite of herself, Cara felt a tiny flicker of interest. Cooking. Every day. For lots and lots of people. It’d be almost like running a restaurant.

She’d always dreamed of doing that.

Still. She shook her head. “That wouldn’t work out. The boys aren’t enjoying camp. I don’t think they’ll be coming back.”

“Oh.” Nick appeared to think that over. “What if they changed their minds?”

“I doubt that’s going to happen.”

“But if it did,” he persisted. “Would you take the job then?”

“It’s not going to happen,” she repeated. “But if they change their minds, I’d be willing to help you out, I suppose.”

She’d only meant to put an end to the conversation, politely. But at her words, a slow smile dawned over Nick’s face—and she frowned.

She remembered his smile. This particular smile especially, because it had always meant one thing.

That Nick had just gotten the better of her.

Laurel Blount lives on a small farm in Georgia with her husband, David, their four children, a milk cow, dairy goats, assorted chickens, an enormous dog, three spoiled cats and one extremely bossy goose with boundary issues. She divides her time between farm chores, homeschooling and writing, and she's happiest with a cup of steaming tea at her elbow and a good book in her hand.

Books by Laurel Blount

Love Inspired

A Family for the Farmer
A Baby for the Minister
Hometown Hope
A Rancher to Trust
Lost and Found Faith
Her Mountain Refuge
Together for the Twins
A Family to Foster
The Triplets' Summer Adventure

Visit the Author Profile page at LoveInspired.com for more titles.

The Triplets' Summer Adventure

LAUREL BLOUNT

Recycling programs for this product may not exist in your area.

ISBN-13: 978-1-335-59747-2

The Triplets' Summer Adventure

For questions and comments about the quality of this book, please contact us at CustomerService@Harlequin.com.

® is a trademark of Harlequin Enterprises ULC.

Love Inspired
22 Adelaide St. West, 41st Floor
Toronto, Ontario M5H 4E3, Canada
www.LoveInspired.com

Printed in Lithuania

A man's heart deviseth his way:
but the Lord directeth his steps.
—*Proverbs* 16:9

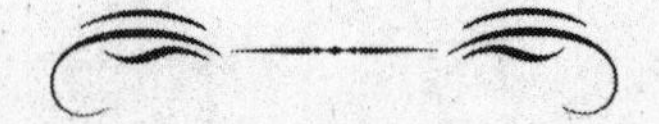

For our beautiful granddaughter Ellie Brock,
who, from the moment of her birth, has sprinkled joy
and love and laughter into all our lives! May God
bless you and keep you always, sweet girl.

Chapter One

"Those sweet children are coming to Red Hawk Camp expecting a nice hot breakfast." Lorna Lipscomb's voice quavered. "And I won't be there to fix it."

"Not your fault," just-for-the-summer park ranger Nick Marshall assured the elderly camp cook for the third time. "You didn't break your leg on purpose." Cradling his phone between his cheek and his shoulder, he scooted boxes and cans around on the pantry shelves.

And sighed. This was not looking good.

"Well, no, but most of these children have missed too many meals already. I can't stand the thought of them going hungry."

In spite of his predicament, Nick smiled. Lorna was a sweet lady. This camp was run on a shoestring, but the people involved were some of the best he'd ever seen.

And he'd seen plenty.

"Don't worry. Nobody's going hungry. I'll find something to feed the kids."

Something. Probably. He just didn't know what. He had fifteen minutes to come up with breakfast for fifty day campers, ages four to eight, and there was nothing in this pantry but canned goods and jumbo bags of flour and sugar.

He didn't need flour and sugar. He needed the world's biggest box of cornflakes.

He also needed to get off the phone, but Lorna was still fretting.

"The doctors say my leg's broken in two places. By the time I'm better, camp will be over. You'll have to find another cook. I'm so sorry."

"We are, too, but we'll figure something out." Nick closed the pantry door and crossed the kitchen to the refrigerator, hoping he'd find something he could manage. Bacon, maybe. He fried bacon like a boss. "Sorry, but I've got to go, Lorna. Everybody here is praying for you, and if there's any way we can help, let us know." He disconnected the call before she started another round of apologies.

As he scanned the contents of the fridge, he sent up a prayer for Lorna's speedy recovery. He tacked on a plea for some sort of fast, kid-friendly breakfast that could be prepared by a guy without much cooking experience.

Because, of course. No bacon.

He shut the refrigerator door and tried to think. Okay. It was just breakfast for a bunch of kids. How hard could that be? He'd promised Lorna he'd figure this out, and he would.

He always figured things out. Sooner or later.

And this dining hall might be short on bacon and cornflakes, but it sure had a great view. The huge, screened windows framed vistas of the Blue Ridge Mountains, dappled with various shades of summer green. The early morning mist lingered in pockets, birds were singing their hearts out, and the whole world looked fresh, innocent and clean.

It looked that way, maybe, from here. But it wasn't. Nick had seen more of the world than most, and he knew it could also be heartbreaking, ruthless and downright scary in places.

He also knew that, in a few minutes, a busload of kids who'd also seen too much of the world's rougher side and who'd normally never have a chance to go to a camp as nice as this one would show up for their second day of healthy food and outdoor fun.

That was a very good thing. He liked being a part of very good things, even when plans went sideways. Which, in his experience, they usually did. That was why he almost never made them.

One thing was for sure. This do-your-brother-a-favor summer job wasn't going to be half as boring as he'd thought.

He hadn't planned on working this summer at all. He'd come home to Cedar Ridge, Georgia, to attend the weddings of not one but two of his foster sisters. He'd just finished working on a construction crew in Ecuador, building some much-needed low-cost housing, and he'd been looking forward to a restful summer of family, food and long, hot showers. He'd only taken the job as Red Hawk State Park's ranger as a favor for his brother Logan.

The former ranger had retired abruptly due to health issues and moved to Florida. Sheriff Logan Carter's office had signed on to cosponsor a summer day camp for local disadvantaged kids at the park, but without a ranger onsite, the outreach was a no-go.

"You'll be home all summer anyway," Logan had pointed out. "What with Jina's wedding at the end of May and then Torey's in August. This will give you something interesting to do. Besides, you've been a ranger before, haven't you?"

He hadn't sounded too sure. Nick's foster family couldn't keep up with his employment. In all honesty, neither could he. His foster mom Ruby said he changed jobs like other people changed socks.

She was exaggerating. Slightly.

But, yeah, he'd worked as a park ranger. Two—no. Three times. He'd also been a bush pilot in Alaska, and a wilderness guide in Montana. He'd worked on crab boats, dairy farms, construction crews and oil rigs. And last year he'd spent six months smuggling medical supplies past some pretty nasty guys in Honduras.

Now *that* had been interesting. Being a park ranger in the tiny mountain town of Cedar Ridge, Georgia? Not so much.

But he'd liked the idea of helping his brother out. He'd missed his family. As much as he loved traveling the world, these people had been his tribe since he'd been grafted into Ruby Sawyer's foster family at age fourteen.

By that time his mom had been dead a year—cancer had taken her at twenty-nine. He'd been heartsick. Bone-deep angry, too. His free-spirited, delightfully irresponsible mom had been more like a sister than a parent, and he'd loathed living in the stodgy foster homes. He'd run away countless times that first year, spending more nights on the streets than in a bed.

After coming to Ruby's, he'd kept a packed knapsack stashed in her goat barn for three months, planning his next escape. But over time, he'd realized that the little mountain farmhouse was different. Bit by bit, Ruby and her five other "hard to place" foster kids had worked their way into Nick's bruised heart.

Finally, one day, he'd walked into the kitchen and wordlessly handed Ruby his battered backpack. Ruby-like, she'd needed no explanation.

Glad you've decided to stay on, son, she'd said. *We've got right attached to you. Now go get washed up. It's near time for supper, and we're having chili. Your favorite.*

From that day on, Ruby and his foster siblings were his people. Maybe he didn't see them all that often, but he loved them with all his heart. So, when his sisters got married, no matter where Nick was or what he was doing, he jumped on a plane and came home.

And when one of them asked him for a favor, he said yes, if he could. Why not? It was only for a few months.

He'd planned on staying largely behind the scenes at the camp, letting the counselors and staff run that part of the show while he kept an eye on the park itself.

That plan wasn't working out so well.

The camp was underfunded and understaffed, and Nick, it turned out, was the official go-to guy for all unassigned problems. There were a lot of those. Today was only day two, and he'd already been pressed to stand in for a counselor who was benched with an impressive case of poison ivy, remove a snake that'd taken up residence in the girls' restroom and clear a fire ant nest out of the camp's well pump.

Now he was on breakfast duty.

He opened the fridge again and delved deeper. Milk. Orange juice. A lot of hot dogs. He reached in, moving things around.

"Nick? What are you doing? Where's the cook?"

His foster brother stood in the doorway, looking concerned. Logan was wearing his sheriff's uniform, so he was likely on his way to work. Apparently he'd made a detour to ensure everything at the camp was going according to plan.

Logan really liked plans. And he knew that Nick really didn't. Hence the check-in.

"In the emergency room. Mrs. Lipscomb tripped over her Pomeranian this morning. She'll be fine, but she broke her leg and is out of commission for the summer."

"What?" Logan came into the kitchen, the screen door slamming shut behind him. "The campers will show up expecting breakfast in..." He glanced at his watch.

"A few minutes. I know. I'm on it." Nick started opening cupboards. Pots, pans. Cans of baked beans. Ah, jam! Grape and strawberry. Score. Now he just needed something to put jam *on*.

"What are you going to do?"

"No idea. Want to run to Angelo's and buy some doughnuts?" Their sister Maggie was co-owner of the local eatery, and she'd help out. But Angelo's was all the way down the mountain in town. He looked at the clock ticking on the log wall. "Better use your sirens."

"I can't." Logan looked agonized.

"You're probably right. A sheriff using his sirens to pick up doughnuts—I definitely see a potential public relations problem."

His brother wasn't amused. "Not what I meant. I have a meeting with the Georgia State Patrol commander this morning." He raked a hand through his short, brown hair. "This isn't good, Nick. We promised to provide the campers with two square meals a day, and some of these kids come from…pretty hard places."

He didn't have to explain what he meant, not to Nick. They both knew way too much about hard places.

"We can't let them go hungry," Logan said. "They have to know they can depend on these meals. That they can depend on us. You know how it is."

Yeah. He did.

"I'll handle it. Go to your meeting."

Logan looked torn. "You're sure you can pull this off?"

Nick shut the cupboard with more force than necessary. "Do you *want* me to lie to you?" It was a rhetorical question. Logan had a thing about lying. "I'm not sure about anything right now, but I'll figure something out." His brother still looked doubtful, so Nick gave him a grin and a wink. "Remember who you're talking to. Trust me, I've dealt with way bigger disasters than this."

"That'd be more comforting if I didn't suspect you caused so many of them," Logan muttered, but his mouth twitched. "All right. I'll try to come back after the meeting and help out. I can't promise, though. It depends on what

I'm dealing with in the county today. Maybe I'd better give Maggie a buzz. She can probably give us some help with lunch, anyway."

"Good idea. See? It's all going to work out."

Logan still didn't look convinced, but he headed outside. As the screen door slapped shut behind him, Nick blew out a long breath.

His brother was right. Maggie would help if she could. He and his foster brothers and sisters always helped each other. But in the meantime, he still had breakfast to deal with.

He scanned the kitchen. He needed something simple. Maybe that jam on some toast? Hadn't he seen packages of bread somewhere?

He was deep in the pantry when he heard the screen door slap again.

"Nick?" his brother called.

"Clock's ticking, bro. If you can't help, at least stop bugging me." Nick stuck his head out of the pantry and stopped short.

Logan wasn't alone. A woman was with him.

"Sorry," he murmured as his brother shot him a look. He glanced at the woman, trying not to stare. She looked familiar, but now that he was back in his hometown, most people did.

This particular woman was blonde and slim. She wore a serious expression and a sedate gray skirt with a white blouse, so probably not associated with the park or the camp. She looked like she was on her way to an office job.

The thought made him shudder, but, hey, he was a live-and-let-live kind of guy. If other people wanted to spend their lives in cubicles, he was fine with it.

The woman looked back with worried eyes that were a

unique shade of green—another tug at old memories. But not only old ones. He'd seen eyes like that recently. Where?

Her hair was shoulder length and super curly—although she'd tried her best to restrain it with hair clasps. The memories tugged harder.

Curly hair. Super-green eyes. That way she studied him without even a hint of a smile. His sense of recognition swelled like a storm cloud.

Good grief. It couldn't be…

"You remember Cara Andrews," Logan said, his voice carefully polite. "Don't you?"

Oh, yeah. Yeah, he sure did.

And suddenly breakfast for fifty was the least of his problems.

"Nick Marshall." Cara murmured her high school enemy's name with a sense of disbelief. "You're not supposed to be here." The words popped out before she could stop them. "Your name wasn't on the staff list."

She was certain of that because she'd read everything she could find about this camp before she'd signed the triplets up. A low-cost summer camp that provided meals, transportation and high-quality outdoor activities? It sounded too good to be true, making Cara instantly suspicious.

Her "too good to be true" ex-husband, Dr. Todd Baker, was the reason her boys qualified for the subsidized camp in the first place. His accountant's fancy footwork had gotten the child support payments down to the bare minimum, and his high-priced lawyer had made veiled threats that if Cara kicked up too much of a fuss, Todd would file for sole custody of the boys.

It was almost certainly a bluff. He didn't want them. He never had. But when it came to her boys, Cara didn't take risks.

So she'd caved, and for the two years since her divorce, money problems kept her nerves on edge. But that was nothing new. She'd been on hyper-alert for so long she'd forgotten how not to worry. The triplets had been born too early, and right from the start, all their complicated care had fallen to Cara. Her fun-loving husband hadn't found fatherhood much fun at all.

What he had found was more and more reasons to work late at his dental office—with the secretary he'd hired to replace Cara after the obstetrician put her on bed rest. Britney was perfect for the job, Todd had assured her. Pleasant, attractive, friendly.

Too good to be true.

So, yes, Cara had double-checked everything about this camp, and Nick's name and photo weren't on the staff list. She'd definitely have noticed. Even back in high school, Nick Marshall had been the kind of guy people noticed, and from what she saw, he hadn't changed much in the past eleven years.

Same sun-streaked, light brown hair with the one lock that flopped over his forehead. Same coffee-brown eyes, same too-handsome-for-his-own-good face, with that aggravating mouth prone to teasing grins. His shoulders were broader than she remembered—that was the only change she could see.

"Nick was a last-minute addition," Logan Carter explained. "Cara needs to talk to somebody about her boys' experience at the camp yesterday," the sheriff went on. "I really do have to get to that meeting, so I'll leave you to it. If that's okay?"

Cara didn't think it was okay at all, but the sheriff was out the door before she could object.

Nick didn't seem happy, either. He shot a narrow-eyed look at his brother's retreating back before turning his attention to her. "It's been a while, Cara. I didn't know you were back in town."

"I haven't been back long." She hoped he wouldn't press for details. Most people did, and reliving her humiliation on a daily basis was getting old. She'd been the valedictorian of their high school class, but she'd dropped out of college to marry Todd. She'd put him through dental school, then managed his office until the boys were born.

Until Britney.

She'd spent the last two years earning her degree online—she'd even gotten her master's. She was putting her life back together, she reminded herself. Bit by bit.

But Nick only shrugged. "Yeah, same here. So, what can I help you with?"

Her relief at his disinterest mingled with annoyance. Of course Nick wouldn't care enough to ask questions. He'd never paid any attention to her unless he was playing some silly prank.

"I enrolled my three boys in the Fledgling group here at camp," she said. "And yesterday—"

That was as far as she got.

"Those triplets!" Nick pointed at her as comprehension dawned on his face. "They're yours!" He laughed and shook his head. "That's been bugging me. I couldn't put my finger on who they reminded me of. It was you! They've got your eyes."

Nick Marshall remembered her eyes? Cara wasn't sure what to think about that—or about the silly flutter that started up in her stomach at the idea.

"The triplets are mine," she confirmed briskly. "And yes, they all have green eyes."

"Not just green." Nick leaned forward, looking into her eyes with such intensity that it felt like he was much closer to her than he actually was. "They're a really interesting color. I never saw the match of them until I was in Peru one September. The hills there are exactly the same color that time of year. Or colors," he went on as if thinking out loud. "Not one green but a dozen different shades all layered together. It's something to see, I'll tell you that. Beautiful."

Oh. Cara's mouth went dry. This was unexpected.

Nobody had paid her a compliment like that in…well. Years. She wasn't sure what to say, so after an awkward second, she circled back to her point. "So, like I said, I wanted to talk to you about my sons. They—"

"I should've guessed. If anybody would have triplets, it'd be you," Nick went on as if she hadn't spoken.

"Excuse me?"

"Back in high school, you always were the poster girl for overachievement."

"That… That has nothing to do with this," she stuttered. "Having triplets…it's not…deliberate."

"It was a joke, Cara." He studied her, a smile curving his mouth. "You haven't changed a bit, have you?"

The casual observation cut through her flustery feelings like a hot knife through butter. Because Nick was wrong. She *had* changed. More than he could possibly imagine.

She'd had no choice. But she wasn't about to explain that to the guy who'd once slipped a live mouse into her purse during Spanish class.

"I didn't drive all the way up this mountain to reminisce about high school, Nick. I came to talk about my boys. They came home crying yesterday."

"Did they?" He didn't seem perturbed—but then again, Nick never did. "Why?"

"The activities were upsetting, and in my opinion, not appropriate for kids their age."

"Is that so? Can you be more specific?"

"I can." She unsnapped her purse and pulled out the list she'd made in the wee small hours last night.

Nick quirked an eyebrow. "You wrote it down?"

His tone was polite, but she heard amusement behind the question. She narrowed her eyes.

"I like to be organized."

"I remember." A chuckle. "All right. I'm listening. Shoot." As he spoke, he stuck his head back into the pantry.

Cara tightened her lips. Typical Nick. She spoke to his back. "First of all, Aaron was handed a cockroach. By a *counselor*." She still couldn't quite believe that.

"Oh, yeah." Nick's voice was muffled, and she could hear rustlings as he moved things around. "I can explain that. They had a special class on bugs yesterday with an entomologist. Really cool. Rats," he muttered. "These are hot dog buns. So much for toast."

"What?"

"Nothing." He stepped out of the pantry and sighed. "Listen, it was a Madagascar hissing cockroach. They're harmless, and the kids washed their hands afterward. Probably."

Probably? She shuddered. "Nonetheless, I'd rather my four-year-old wasn't forced to handle them."

"Nonetheless." Nick repeated the word solemnly, but she heard that whiff of amusement again. "Was he forced? I mean, did he tell the counselor he didn't want to hold it?"

"I'm not sure," she admitted. "Aaron can be a little shy sometimes."

"Well, no worries. I'll give the counselor a heads-up. He's a nice guy, so I'm sure he had no idea he was upsetting anybody. Anyway, it was the first day for him, too. Bound to be a few hiccups." He laughed. "More than a few. Where are your boys, by the way? Aren't they coming to camp today?"

"They're riding the bus in." She'd considered bringing them with her, but after careful consideration, she'd decided against that. The boys needed to get used to riding the bus. It was going to be a necessity in the fall, when she started her new job teaching remedial math at the college where her father worked. The bus had been one important checkmark in the pro-camp column—they'd get that experience before pre-K started.

Besides, she'd preferred to have this conversation privately. She didn't want to air her concerns in front of the boys. They were unhappy enough as it was.

The truth was, they'd been unhappy ever since the move. She'd hoped their sadness would pass. Instead it seemed to be settling in, and that worried her.

A lot.

The books she'd read—and she'd read plenty—had suggested fresh air, sunshine and friendly companionship. This very low-cost camp had seemed like the answer to her prayers, but so far it was only making things worse.

"Look," Nick was saying, "I wouldn't worry about one bad day. Correct me if I'm wrong, but your boys haven't spent much time outside before this. Right?"

She blinked. "How do you know that?"

"Well." He coughed. "They showed up to camp wearing polo shirts and ironed khakis, for one thing. And they acted like they'd never seen a lizard before. Totally freaked out when one ran across the table at lunchtime."

That lizard had been another topic of tearful discussion last night, and it was point number two on her list. "About that—"

"Look." Nick glanced at his watch. "I'd love to talk more about this, but I've got a crisis to deal with. The camp cook is out with an injury, and a horde of hungry kids are showing up for breakfast in just a few minutes. I'm pinch-hitting, which seems to be my job description around here, and I've got no idea what I'm supposed to feed them. So—"

"Pancakes," Cara informed him impatiently. She didn't like having her concerns waved aside. And if he could interrupt, so could she.

"What?"

"Pancakes are on the menu today. Pancakes, orange wedges and sausage patties."

He frowned at her. "How do you know that?"

She frowned back. "The menus were on the information sheet. And the website."

"Oh." Nick ran a hand through his dark hair, standing it on end. "Pancakes," he repeated. "I'm supposed to make pancakes for fifty kids."

"It won't be that hard. They're quick and easy, and you've got a big griddle over there." She nodded at the gigantic stove hulking in the corner of the log building. "Although you'd better get busy mixing up your batter if you plan to have them ready anytime soon."

"Batter. Right. Um. You don't happen to know how to mix up a gigantic batch of pancake batter, do you?"

"It's exactly the same as mixing up a small batch. You just multiply everything." When he kept staring at her, she made an impatient noise. "It's just math, Nick."

"Math was never my best subject. And I'm not too good at cooking, either." He gave her a hopeful smile. "You were always great at math, as I recall. How are you at making pancakes?"

Oh, for pity's sake. He couldn't be serious. "Are you asking me to help you make breakfast?" She shook her head. "Nick—"

"You wouldn't only be helping me. You don't want all those kids to go hungry, do you? Or worse, eat pancakes made by a guy who can't do double-digit multiplication in his head? Besides," he added with a wink, "you can run down the rest of your list of complaints while you cook."

Cara hesitated. On the one hand, this was typical Nick. He was a genius at charming people into doing what he wanted them to do—and she'd been suckered more than once before she'd wised up.

On the other hand, her boys were really looking forward to this particular meal. Sugary breakfasts were a rarity for them, and the prospect of those pancakes had enticed them onto the bus this morning. She whuffed out a sigh. "Oh, all right. But you're helping."

"Of course." Nick bowed. "I'm at your service, Chef."

Chef. The word took her by surprise. She'd once dreamed of becoming a chef. Back years ago, when she'd still believed any dream could come true if you just tried hard enough.

Now she knew better.

She studied him sternly.

"Do you want my help or not?" she asked. He nodded. "Then stop being silly and get me an apron. And a really, really big bowl."

Chapter Two

By the time Nick had Cara squared away in the kitchen, bus brakes were screeching outside. The kids had arrived, and breakfast wasn't even close to ready.

Through the huge, screened windows, he watched the campers spilling from the bus. They'd be here any minute, expecting food.

Cara muttered to herself as she struggled with the canvas apron he'd tossed to her. "Good grief, this thing goes all the way to the floor. Who cooked here last, Bigfoot?" She finally got it on—sort of—and pulled the straps around to tie in the front. Then she began rolling up the sleeves of her white blouse, deliberately, neatly.

And slowly.

Nick fought back his impatience. Cara, he remembered, had always been like this. No matter what task she was working on, she had one speed. Granny gear.

It had driven him bonkers when they'd been paired up on class projects because he was the exact opposite. He hated standing around doing nothing. Jump in and sort things out later was his motto. He glanced out the window again. The counselors were organizing the kids into their groups, preparing to bring them to the dining hall.

"You get started. I'll see if I can stall them. Be back in a minute."

Sleeves dealt with, Cara had bent to study the dials on

the industrial-size stove. "You better be," she called as he sprinted out the door.

When he jogged back into the dining hall half an hour later, she was still at the stove. But now, he noticed with relief, there was a smell of sausage in the air.

Things must be moving along.

"Good news! I bought us some more time."

Cara didn't turn around. "I'd certainly hope so. That was the longest minute in human history."

"Sorry. It wasn't easy," Nick said. "The counselors weren't thrilled about having to freestyle an activity for a crew of hungry kids. I helped set up an obstacle course out by the lake. That'll keep them busy for a while. How's it going in here?"

She tested the griddle with a flick of water. "Not quite ready. But close." Her lips were pursed into a thoughtful pout that hit his stomach with a jolt of recognition.

Cara's thinking face. He used to tease her about that. Once he'd snapped a photo of her looking like that at her chemistry book, which he'd blown up and put on the front page of the school newspaper. She'd been furious—and he'd been confused.

What was there to be mad about? So, she looked a little silly. But it was also pretty cute.

He'd never understood Cara Andrews.

"Are you just going to stand there, or are you going to help?" She flicked another drop of water on the griddle.

He blinked. "I'll help. If you'll walk me through it, I could mix up the—oh." He stopped short. A jumbo bowl of batter was already at her elbow, and there was more in a pitcher beside the griddle, ready for pouring. "Wow. Never mind. You've been busy."

"Efficient," she corrected. "I'll handle the pancakes. The sausage patties were in the freezer. They're precooked, so they're thawing out in the oven. You can slice up the oranges and get the plates and cups ready."

"Aye, aye, Captain." He gave her a sassy salute, which she pointedly ignored. She flicked another drop of water onto the griddle, and this time it sizzled promisingly. "You sure you don't need any help with those? You're going to have to make a lot, you know."

"Two hundred should do it, I think."

"Two *hundred*?"

"Three apiece for each child and the staff members." She spared him a quick glance. "And a good many to spare. I figured some kids might come extra hungry."

"You figured right. These kids are all from struggling families so—" He broke off, remembering that Cara's kids had qualified for the camp, too.

That surprised him a little—but only a little. Life took rough detours sometimes, and nobody was immune to that, not even chronic overachievers like Cara.

He cut a wary look at her to see if she was insulted. Her cheeks were pink, but he couldn't tell if that was embarrassment or the heat from the griddle.

"I know," she said quietly. "Two hundred pancakes may seem wasteful, but I thought under the circumstances, it'd be better to have too many than to run short."

"It doesn't seem wasteful to me. Ambitious. But not wasteful." He watched as she poured batter on the griddle in perfect little circles. "That's really smart, using a pitcher."

It wasn't much of an olive branch, but it was the best he could come up with on the spur of the moment.

"It's the fastest way when you have a lot to do. I cook for triplets, remember? Speaking of that," she went on. "You have a lot of oranges to cut up. You'd better get started."

"Okay." She'd given him the easy job. Chopping oranges was a cinch compared with making a million pancakes.

That was Cara. She'd been the same way in school. She'd never trusted anybody but herself with the hardest jobs, and arguing with her didn't do much good.

Not that he planned to argue, not today, anyway. He grabbed the net bags of oranges he'd spotted in the pantry and set them on the butcher block counter.

When he reached for a knife, Cara made a sharp sound. "You need to clean that surface first."

Nick paused, the knife in his hand. "What? You mean wipe down the counter?" He looked at it. "It's clean. Mrs. Lipscomb scrubbed the whole kitchen yesterday after lunch."

"It may look clean but that doesn't mean it is." Cara lifted an edge of pancake with her spatula. "No telling what scurried over it during the night. This place is very—" she shuddered "—rustic."

Nick laughed, then tried to cover it with a cough. "This is a camp," he pointed out. "Rustic is kind of a requirement."

The cough hadn't fooled her. She shot him a narrow look. "Well, dirty isn't. There's disinfectant spray under the sink. Wash the oranges, too. There's no time to peel them, so you'll have to serve them in wedges."

"They're not eating the peel, Cara."

"Maybe not, but they'll have the peel right at their mouths, so the oranges should be clean. It won't take long. Fill the sink with water and squirt in some dishwashing liquid. Plop the oranges in, jiggle them around and then rinse them off well."

Oh, come on. This was camp. The kids would be covered with dirt by the end of the day, so he saw no reason to be concerned about a speck or two on an orange peel.

On the other hand, Cara was doing him a favor. A really big one, in spite of the fact that he'd never been her favorite person. The least he could do was let her boss him around.

"Fine."

He followed her instructions. She didn't say anything, appearing totally absorbed in flipping the first batch of pancakes. But he saw her sneaking glances, checking to make sure that he was doing what he was supposed to.

Boy, did that feel familiar. She'd always been like that in high school, too. Big on everybody following rules, even the ones that didn't make sense.

That had bugged him—partly because he was a strong believer in tweaking rules when necessary. Thanks to his hippie-throwback of a mom, he wasn't much on blind obedience. Maybe they'd only had thirteen years together before she'd passed away, but Leah Marshall had left a lasting impression. She'd taught her son to live life to the fullest and to measure rules against his values before deciding how strictly to follow them.

She'd also stressed accepting all kinds of people. *God has a different purpose for everybody,* she'd told him. *So of course, He gives people different personalities. Takes all kinds to make a world.*

He was sure she'd tell him that included orange-scrubbing, rule-following math whizzes.

Not that he'd ever had much trouble accepting Cara. He'd gotten irritated with her now and then, sure. And she'd definitely gotten aggravated with him a few times.

Okay, more than a few times.

They were night-and-day different, Cedar Ridge High School was small, and they couldn't exactly avoid each other. The truth was, he'd enjoyed pushing Cara's buttons and watching those eyes spit green sparks in his direction. It was the only time she ever paid much attention to him, and in spite of their differences, something about her drew him.

Looking back, he figured he'd probably had a little crush on her. Definitely a one-sided thing, and it had petered out quick. Plenty of other girls had liked him just fine, and he wasn't one to linger long in front of a closed door.

What was the point? Better to move on.

He scrubbed down the wooden counter—and the knife for good measure—and washed the oranges. He'd barely started slicing before she was layering yet another mound of hot pancakes onto the big platter she'd tucked next to the sausages in the warming oven. He'd lost count of how many she'd made already.

Before she could slide it back in the oven, he snitched a pancake, earning himself a sharp look.

"Taste test," he explained with a wink.

He kept his tone light, but he wasn't kidding. It had occurred to him that he didn't know anything about Cara's cooking abilities. As long as the food was edible, it would be fine. But he'd better at least check it before serving it to a bunch of unsuspecting kids.

He folded the pancake, took a bite—and froze.

"This is good," he mumbled through a mouthful. He chewed and swallowed. "I mean really, really good."

Cara threw him a sideways glance. He must have looked sincere because her shoulders relaxed. "Thanks."

"Seriously. They're way better than mine." They were. Lighter, fluffier and with a subtle flavor he couldn't quite place. Nutmeg, maybe? He wasn't savvy enough about spices to be sure.

"What do you mean *yours*?" Cara whirled, brandishing the spatula. "You said you didn't know how to make pancakes!" She swatted him on the arm.

"Ouch! I don't! Not like these. I've made 'em from a boxed mix, for myself, over a campfire. Not hundreds from scratch for fifty kids. Seriously, no idea how to do that. None. Okay? Lower your weapon."

She studied him suspiciously, spatula poised. He offered a cheesy grin.

"I can't believe you just hit me with a spatula," he said. "Maybe you *have* changed some since high school."

"I have. And don't you forget it." She stalked to the sink and made a point of washing the spatula. Then she returned to the griddle, still looking annoyed.

"Well, you're obviously the best person for the job because that's the best pancake I ever ate. Where'd you learn to cook like that?"

"You don't have to flatter me." Cara didn't take her eyes off the current batch of pancakes. "I've already agreed to do this, so I'll do it."

"I'm not flattering you," Nick said, exasperated. "I'm paying you an honest compliment and asking you an honest question."

Cara's expression shifted, and for a second he thought she was going to say something. But she didn't get the chance.

They both heard the thundering roar at the same time. A quick glance at the clock confirmed Nick's fears.

The time he'd bought them had run out.

"The kids," he said. "They're coming."

"Fine." Cara calmly flipped the batch of circles on the griddle, then reached into the stove to remove pans of sausage and a huge, heaping platter of fluffy pancakes. "I'm just about done."

Nick surveyed the mountain of uncut oranges with some alarm. "I'm not. And I still haven't set out the plates and cups."

He expected a snarky remark, but Cara simply continued arranging the pans and platters on the buffet as the roar grew louder. "Where are they?"

"What? The kids? Not far."

She rolled her eyes. "The plates and cups."

"In that cupboard there beside the fridge."

Without a word, she retrieved the supplies and started setting them out. She finished just as the first kids barreled through the door.

Nick redoubled his slicing efforts, feeling guilty. He'd been given the easy job, and he still hadn't been able to keep up.

He should have seen that coming. This was Cara Andrews. She might've changed in some ways since high school. So had he. But one thing hadn't changed.

She could still show him up without breaking a sweat.

In spite of what Nick had promised, they hadn't talked about her list of concerns at all, Cara realized. Of course, it probably wouldn't have done much good if they had.

Men like Nick Marshall, handsome, charming, the-rules-don't-apply-to-me men, they caused problems. They didn't solve them.

Even though he hadn't kept his end of the bargain—big surprise—she'd finish helping with breakfast because she'd said she would. Unlike Nick and her ex-husband, Cara believed in keeping her word, even when it was difficult.

So she patiently helped a long line of excited kids put syrup on their pancakes, trying her best to minimize the mess. It wasn't easy. Syrup and kids were a recipe for a sticky disaster.

Nick was still slicing oranges. He'd fill up the bowl with wedges and then duck behind the counter to cut more while the kids emptied it.

She had to give him credit. He was working fast enough that the supply met the demand. Barely.

When her three sons made it to the front of the line, their eyes were wide.

"What're you doing here, Mama?" Brian whispered. "Did you come to take us home? Please?"

"Are you s'posed to be doing this?" Aaron asked. He was her worrier. "You could get in trouble."

"Can I have lotsa syrup?" Scott asked hopefully. She tried to limit the boys' sugar intake to a healthy level, and syrup and pancakes were a rare treat.

Although the triplets looked alike, they had very distinct personalities. Sadly, today all three had something in common. She saw evidence of tears on their freckled faces.

Her heart sank. They hadn't even had breakfast yet, and they'd already been crying. Not good.

She forced a cheerful smile. "Surprise! I'm helping because the cook's out sick. Isn't that fun?"

"No." Brian said flatly, and his brothers shook their heads. "Nothing's fun here. We wanna go home."

"You said we could," Scott reminded her. "If we didn't like camp today."

"We don't," Aaron whispered firmly.

"Today's not over yet, boys. Our deal was that you'd give camp one more good try. Tell you what," she said recklessly, "you can each have extra syrup." She plied the bottle generously over their plates. "Just try not to get it on your shirts. Here, wait a second." Quickly she unfolded three napkins and tucked them into the boys' collars. "There. Now, go sit down and eat. But walk slowly, okay?"

She wished she could carry the plates for them. Fine motor skills had been a little delayed—not uncommon with twins or triplets. They were catching up, but—

"Hey, lady, can I have some syrup?" the next child prompted impatiently.

"Of course. Sorry." She plopped a generous amount on his stack. The kid behind him elbowed his neighbor and laughed.

"Lookit them kids over there wearing bibs like babies."

Cara caught her breath in horror. She looked at her sons, hoping they hadn't overheard. But they had. Brian's face crumpled. He pulled his napkin out of his shirt and wadded it up, Scott ducked his head down, focusing on his plate, and Aaron's mouth wobbled dangerously.

"Those aren't bibs." Nick appeared beside her, sliding another juicy avalanche of oranges into the big metal bowl. "It's a way to keep the sticky syrup off their shirts so the yellow jackets and the ants won't bug 'em. Smart, if you ask me. I mean…unless you like being dive-bombed by yellow jackets, Parker." Nick tucked a napkin in the collar of his uniform, then reached over the counter and tousled the boy's hair, making a buzzing noise.

"I ain't afraid of bugs," the boy protested with a grin.

"I didn't think about insects," Cara whispered as the boy walked away. "Maybe I shouldn't have given them all so much syrup."

"That was what you call a distraction, Cara," Nick muttered under his breath. "See? Nobody's thinking about bibs anymore."

Cara blinked. It was true. Her sons, napkins now out of sight, were huddled together at a table, eating their pancakes. The places beside them had filled up with other kids, but nobody was teasing them. They didn't look happy, but they weren't crying. That was something.

"Oh," she murmured. "Thanks."

Nick winked, then returned to his slicing.

The kids ate fast. The last camper was barely through the line before a group gathered at the trash can to dispose of their empty plates. Then they headed outside where the camp counselors were waiting, clipboards in hand and whistles at the ready.

However, as soon as her sons had dumped their sticky

plates in the trash, they headed in the opposite direction—straight to her. She knew what was coming, and she sighed.

She wasn't sure how much more of this she could take today. She'd had a struggle to get them on the bus this morning. They hadn't trusted her suggestion that camp might be more fun today.

She supposed she couldn't exactly blame them, not after the way she'd oversold their move to Cedar Ridge. Like this camp, living with their grandfather wasn't living up to her glowing descriptions.

It wasn't his fault. A quiet and bookish man, Professor John Andrews would have found living with one four-year-old challenging. Three all at once, all day long? That was a lot for her poor dad to handle, but he was trying his best.

"Do we *have* to stay, Mommy?" Aaron dragged the toe of his shoe against the rough-plank floor. "We don't like it here."

"We rode the bus." Scott was the bargainer of the trio. "We didn't wanna, but we did. Can't we go home now?"

Brian said nothing. He wouldn't ask to go home again because she'd already said no, but she could read the silent plea on his face. Like his mom, he believed in following rules, but he was just as miserable as his brothers.

She made herself smile. "We all agreed to give camp one more try, didn't we? So we'll see how you like it after today."

"We ain't gonna like it any better than yesterday," Brian warned. "We can already tell."

Cara sighed and surrendered. "Then you won't have to come back after today. Okay?"

Maybe she should give up and take them home. Her father wouldn't be happy. He'd been so relieved at the prospect of having a triplet-free home for most of the summer. He was working on an article for some scholarly journal and preparing for his autumn classes, and he was craving peace and quiet.

"Come on, guys." Nick appeared beside them. "I'll walk you to the assembly hall so you can rejoin the Fledglings." He had his ball cap on backward, and he looked remarkably relaxed, considering the mad scramble they'd just been through.

The boys looked up at him uncertainly. "Go ahead." Cara forced a cheery note into her voice. "I'll be here awhile cleaning up the kitchen." Maybe they'd feel better if they knew she was here at the camp, too.

"I'll handle that," Nick told her. "I've got to come back anyway to figure out lunch. I'll get everything squared away then." He held out a hand. She accepted it, his warm, strong fingers closing over hers. "You've been a big help, Cara, and I appreciate it. I'm sorry we didn't get more of a chance to go over your…uh…list, but I can give you my number if you want to call me after hours."

"Don't worry about it," she said with a sigh. "I don't think the list's going to matter after today."

He studied her, his eyes thoughtful. But all he said was, "Okay. Let's get going, guys. You don't want to miss today's assembly. We're having a birds of prey show."

Aaron shot his mother a frantic look. He didn't like birds much better than he liked cockroaches. Before she could speak, Brian put his arm around his brother's shoulders.

"Don't worry," the little boy said with a sigh. "I'll take care of you."

As they trudged off with Nick, Cara fought the urge to cry. She should have known this promising camp would turn out to be another disappointment. She couldn't remember the last time something had gone right. No matter how carefully she planned things out, everything in her life kept going wrong.

She looked around the disheveled kitchen. Nick had said she didn't have to clean up, that he'd handle it. But he was already juggling the problem of the missing cook on top of whatever his usual job was. Besides, kids were messy eaters and Nick wasn't the most detail-oriented guy. If crumbs and food bits were left here they'd attract ants.

Or worse.

And since the only thing waiting for her back at her father's house was more disappointment, she might as well do another good deed and clean the place up.

She was sweeping the floor with a bedraggled broom she'd found in a supply closet when Nick poked his head in the door an hour later.

"You're still here?" He looked around and whistled. "Cara, you didn't have to do all this."

"I didn't mind. It's not like I have anything else to do today." She spoke honestly before she thought, and then flushed. "I don't start my teaching job until the fall, and since the boys are here for the day, I'm at loose ends."

"Really." Nick perched on the edge of a table. "Well, in that case…" He offered a bright, winning smile—and suspicion tickled up her backbone.

Uh-oh.

"What?" she asked.

"Would you consider taking on the camp cook job for the summer? It doesn't pay much, and it's not…you know…prestigious or anything. But if you're really at loose ends, and since your boys will be here anyway… What do you say?"

In spite of herself, Cara felt a tiny flicker of interest. Cooking. Every day. For lots and lots of people. It'd be almost like running a restaurant.

She'd always dreamed of doing that.

Still. She shook her head. "That wouldn't work out."

"I know you're not a professional cook, but you sure did a bang-up job today. And we wouldn't expect fancy meals. Whatever you can rustle up would be fine. It would be a huge help—not just to me," he added quickly. "For the kids, too."

"I didn't say no because I couldn't handle the job." She could so totally handle the job, and it stung that Nick would assume otherwise. "The boys aren't enjoying camp. I don't think they'll be coming back."

"Oh." Nick appeared to think that over. "What if they changed their minds and decided they liked camp?"

"I doubt that's going to happen."

"But if it did," he persisted. "Would you take the job then?"

Cara sighed. This was a pointless conversation. Once the triplets made up their minds they didn't like something, they were virtually impossible to sway. Goodness knows, she'd tried.

"It's not going to happen," she repeated. "But if they change their minds, I'd be willing to help you out, I suppose."

She'd only meant to put an end to the conversation, politely. But at her words a slow smile dawned over Nick's face—and she frowned.

Nick had remembered her eyes from high school. Well, she remembered his smile. This particular smile especially because it had always meant the same thing.

That Nick had just gotten the better of her.

Chapter Three

"You're *sure* you want to go back to the camp?" Cara asked for the third time. She, her dad and the boys sat in her father's bookcase-lined dining room, eating a supper of pot roast with vegetables and homemade biscuits. "All of you?"

"Yeth!" Brian affirmed around a mouthful of food. He caught his mother's expression and swallowed before speaking again. "We love camp!"

"This morning you hated it." She ignored the nervous cough from her dad's end of the table. He clearly wished she'd leave well enough alone.

Well, she wasn't going to. Not until she got to the bottom of this sudden shift in her sons' attitudes.

"What changed your minds?"

"Ranger Nick." Scott's eyes lit up. "He's fun, and he tells good stories, and he knows how to do all kinds of stuff! Before he took us back to the Fledglings, he showed us how to skip rocks on the lake."

"Before the bird assembly? Right after you left breakfast?"

Before Nick had come back and got her to agree to take on the cooking job—if her sons decided to stay at camp.

All three boys nodded.

"Brian's rock skipped six times," Aaron said.

"My rocks just plopped at first, but Ranger Nick helped me, and then they skipped!" Brian said happily.

"I see." Cara stabbed a piece of roast.

Her boys might be Nick's biggest fans, but she wasn't. As she'd suspected when she'd recognized that grin on his face, she'd been bamboozled.

"Tomorrow he's gonna take us on the lake." Brian bounced in his seat. "And we get to ride in a boat. He promised. So we like camp now."

"And you really want to go every day? For the whole summer?"

Her father cleared his throat again. "They've said they do, Cara. Numerous times. I believe we can consider the matter settled. And possibly dinner over with." He looked with some concern at Scott, who was crafting a sculpture out of mashed potatoes and roasted carrots.

"Looks like somebody's had enough to eat," she observed. "Boys, why don't you go to your room and play for a while before bedtime?"

"Thanks for supper, Mama." Brian pushed his chair back and climbed down off the dictionary serving as a makeshift booster seat.

"It was good," Aaron whispered as he followed suit.

"But it woulda been better with no vegtubbles," Scott said as he bounced out of his chair.

The boys disappeared up the steps. Seconds later, a series of thumps sounded overhead.

Her father looked up at the ceiling, his eyebrows raised. "Listen to that."

"Sorry, Dad," Cara murmured. "I'll remind them about not running in the house."

"No, my dear." He looked at her over his reading glasses. "I'm remarking on the change in their behavior. I haven't seen them so energetic since you all arrived."

Cara studied the ceiling thoughtfully. A heavy thud made the light fixture wiggle. It was followed by a shriek of boyish laughter.

When was the last time she'd heard her boys laughing like that?

Not for a long time.

"It seems that summer camp agrees with them after all," her father said. "But it doesn't appear to agree with you, although, as I recall, it was your suggestion in the first place."

Cara hesitated, then decided to be honest. "The Ranger Nick they keep talking about? It's Rick Marshall." Her father lifted his eyebrows, waiting for further information. "We went to high school together."

"I see. And?"

"And we didn't exactly get along." She stood and began gathering up the dishes.

Her father poured himself a cup of coffee while he considered that information. John Andrews always weighed his words and thought things through.

"Do you fear for the boys' safety with this man?"

"Oh, no." The answer came with a certainty that surprised her. It was the truth, she realized. She didn't fear for her boys with Nick. "He's not dangerous. He's just… annoying. Back in high school, he was always up to something. Playing tricks, embarrassing people. He never met a rule he wouldn't bend, but he got away with it because everybody liked him. Even the teachers. No matter what he does, somehow or another he always manages to come out on top." Unlike her. She hadn't seen the top in so long she probably wouldn't recognize it. "Like today. The boys had made it plain that they hated camp. So when Nick wanted me to take the job as camp cook—"

"Camp cook?" Her father set down his coffee cup with a clink. "You?"

"I *can* cook, Dad," she retorted over her shoulder as she carried the first load of dishes into the kitchen.

Her father's voice drifted after her. "You cook very well. But you also have a master's degree in mathematics."

She returned to the table and began collecting silverware. "Nick doesn't know that. Although it probably wouldn't have mattered if he had. He's in a pinch because the woman who was supposed to do the cooking broke her leg. Anyway, after I helped him deal with breakfast, and he'd walked the boys back to their group, he asked me to consider cooking for the whole summer. I told him I couldn't because the boys had decided camp wasn't for them. Nick asked if I'd reconsider if they changed their minds. I said I would, but—"

"Why would you say such a thing?"

"You're missing the point, Dad."

"Which is?"

"Nick had already convinced the boys to continue with camp before he offered me the job. He tricked me." She felt a flush of annoyance at the thought. It was embarrassing to remember how he'd played her.

"He lied to you?"

"Well, no," she admitted. "Not…exactly." That was the thing about Nick. You never could pin down anything he'd actually done wrong, but somehow he always ended up getting his way.

Her father thought this over. "You wanted the boys to enjoy camp, didn't you?" She nodded. "Then it seems this man's interference was actually helpful. Unless you dislike the idea of cooking for the camp."

"No," she said slowly. "I…don't dislike the idea."

Her father shook his head, but he shrugged. "Well, you are rather at loose ends until fall semester begins. This would give you something to do. Besides, this way you'll be at the camp if the boys need you. All in all, this seems like a fairly satisfactory—albeit surprising—arrangement."

As she carried more dishes into the kitchen, she noticed a relieved expression on her dad's face. Maybe the boys weren't the only ones her father would be happy to have out of the house for the summer.

Not that she blamed him. Her dad had a generous heart, and he hadn't hesitated when she'd asked if she and the boys could move home so she could save money. He'd even pulled strings to get her the teaching job at his university.

But he was a quiet, studious man, used to living alone with his books. Adding four people to his household hadn't been easy for him.

When she came back into the dining room, she patted him on the shoulder. "I'll handle the dishes by myself tonight, Dad. Why don't you take your coffee into the study and work on your paper?"

Her father's eyes lit up. "If you're sure you don't mind, I think I will." He gathered up his coffee and shuffled off in the direction of his cluttered study.

Once the kitchen was put to rights, Cara collected laundry from the dryer. Then she climbed the steps to the second floor, pausing to peek at the boys, playing in their big bedroom.

Deep in some game involving superhero figures, they didn't notice her. She smiled at their animated chatter as they crawled around on the rug. Her father was right. The boys seemed happier tonight than they had in a very long time.

She'd take the camp cook job, she decided as she went to her own bedroom to fold the laundry. She didn't like being tricked into it by Nick, but her dad had made some good points. This way she could also give her overwhelmed father the blessing of a quiet summer, and the idea of preparing meals for a crew of hungry campers sounded kind of…fun.

It had been a long time since she had done something fun.

She just hoped all the wildlife stayed outside and behaved itself. If Nick wanted her help, he'd better behave himself, too. No more tricks. This wasn't high school, and she wasn't putting up with any of his nonsense.

First thing tomorrow she'd make sure he understood that.

The next morning just before dawn, Nick awoke from a sound sleep to hear somebody rustling around in his kitchen.

Since by the smell of it, that person was also making coffee, he closed his eyes again and smiled. It had to be Ruby, though why she'd come over this early was anybody's guess.

When he'd come home, Ruby had insisted he bunk in the old family cabin. It was just up the mountain from her farmhouse and had been vacant since Logan and Charlotte had built their home on the outskirts of town.

The arrangement suited him. Close enough to Ruby that he could spend plenty of time with her, but far enough away that he had his privacy.

Well. Usually.

He sat up, ran one hand through his hair and reached for his phone. The first thing he saw was a message from Cara, agreeing to take the camp cook job.

"Yes!" He pumped a triumphant fist. One problem solved. Half a million to go.

"You awake?" Ruby called from the kitchen. "Good. Get in here before I drink all this coffee myself."

Nick threw off the covers and stretched. This day was off to an excellent start. "Coming."

In the kitchen, he found Ruby holding a coffee mug in one hand and wiping the counters with the other. But slowly, not with her usual energy. He felt a twinge of worry.

"Sit down, Ruby. I can do my own cleaning."

"Don't look like it. You keep leaving crumbs out overnight, you're gonna draw varmints."

"Already did." He kissed the top of her gray head. "But since she made coffee, I'm in no particular hurry to get rid of her."

Ruby chuckled and swatted his arm before passing him a mug. "Made it strong enough to dissolve the spoon, just like you like it."

He accepted it with a grateful sigh and dropped into a handy chair. "Thanks. I need this more than you know."

Ruby poured herself a second cup, diluted it generously with milk and took the seat across from him at the small kitchen table. "You mean to tell me that running a little old day camp for kids is wearing out an adventure hound like you?"

"This job's not as easy as it sounded." Nick took his first ambrosial sip of coffee. "By the end of the day yesterday I was dog-tired."

"You? Tired?" Ruby snorted. "You're usually a bundle of energy. You getting old?"

"Feels that way sometimes." He took another grateful sip of coffee and flexed his left shoulder, the one he'd shattered four years ago trying to rescue a stranded hiker on an icy mountain trail. It was aching, which probably meant rain later today.

He didn't have many aches and pains, thankfully. Just the shoulder so far, and a knee that he couldn't trust on long hikes unless he brought along a brace. He shrugged off the twinges philosophically. They were souvenirs from spectacular adventures, and to Nick's way of thinking, well worth it.

"Small wonder." Ruby studied him over the rim of her coffee cup. "You never stay still long enough to rest yourself."

"I don't like staying still."

"Oh, you'll always be a wanderer—you're made that way. But a grown man does better when he has a home of his own to come back to. And," she added, a mischievous twinkle in her hazel eyes, "somebody special to share it with."

So that's where this was going. Nick's foster brothers and sisters had warned him that Ruby had taken to matchmaking in her old age. Now that Jina was freshly married and Torey about to follow suit, he was Ruby's last remaining holdout.

"My home is wherever you are, Ruby," he reminded her. "Remember? You told me that when I first came here."

"I remember." She patted his arm and sighed. "But I ain't gonna be around forever, Nicky."

A chilly fist closed around his heart. "Are you feeling all right?" They'd all been worried about Ruby. She'd had a series of dizzy spells, and she'd even ended up briefly hospitalized last fall. Logan had privately expressed concern to Nick just the other day.

All this fuss over the weddings, coming so close together. I'm afraid Ruby won't be up to it.

Are you kidding? Nick had answered. *All the wedding stuff may give us the shivers, but Ruby'll eat it up. Wait and see.*

She'd glowed with happiness at Jina's wedding two weeks ago, so he'd figured he was right. But he'd noticed her moving slower, not eating so well. Maybe—

"I'm fit as a fiddle," she assured him. "Just getting old. Ain't no cure for that. I have to say, I'm surprised you ain't already found yourself a sweetheart. All them places you've been, a good-lookin' charmer like you." His foster mom tilted her head like a curious bird. "You're telling me no woman's ever caught your eye?"

Nick stalled by lifting his coffee mug back to his mouth. Sure, women had caught his eye. Plenty of times.

But none had ever laid a finger on his heart.

"You're a hard act to follow," he said finally. "Anyway,

I've got all the family I need. I'm just not the marrying kind."

"Phhth." Ruby made a dismissive noise. "You're not the staying-put kind, but that's different. There's girls that like to travel just as much as you do. Find yourself one of those."

As usual, there was a germ of truth in Ruby's observation. He liked to keep moving. Everything stayed easy that way. And yeah, there were probably women who liked the same kind of lifestyle.

He wasn't ruling out the idea of finding somebody like that. Someday. Maybe.

But not yet.

"Is this why you broke in here at dark-thirty in the morning, Ruby? To pester me about getting married?"

Ruby's mouth curved into a smile. "Ain't breaking in if you got a key. And I notice I'm not hearing any complaints about this coffee. No, I was wondering how you're planning to get along without Lorna. I heard tell she's broken her leg. What are you going to do about feeding all those young 'uns?"

"I've already solved that problem." He recounted the morning's adventure with Cara while Ruby sipped her coffee.

"Sounds like God's working things out," she said when he'd finished.

"He sure is. Those pancakes were incredible. Cara's as good a cook as Maggie." Maybe better, at least when it came to pancakes, but brotherly loyalty kept him from saying so.

"I'm not only talking about the pancakes, son. Cara's got them three little boys to look after, and she's been through a real hard time, what with her marriage breaking up and all. Cooking at the camp might be a good distraction, and she'll make a little money, too."

Nick frowned. "What kind of hard time? I mean, I know she's divorced, but I never heard what happened."

"That ain't my story to tell. But don't you aggravate that girl, you hear? I know how you like to tease, but she's got a lot on her plate, and I imagine she's feeling pretty shaky just now."

Shaky? Cara? Hard to imagine that. She'd always been so cool and confident.

He shrugged. "I'll try to stay on her good side, but Cara's never liked me too much."

Ruby waved her hand. "Oh, she just never really got to know you. Once she does, that'll change, and you'll get along fine." Then she frowned. "But maybe you'd better use the dimmer switch on that charm of yours, son. The last thing Cara needs right now is to get her heart broken."

Nick choked on a mouthful of coffee. For once, his mom didn't have a clue what she was talking about. Cara wouldn't let him within ten miles of her heart.

"Just how irresistible do you think I am, Ruby?"

"When you put your mind to it? You could charm a bird right out of a tree. Course," his foster mom went on dryly, "if it had any sense, it'd peck you on the head."

Nick got up, pulled Ruby up out of her chair and enveloped her in a big hug. "Ruby, you have a bad habit of meddling in people's personal lives, but I wouldn't trade you for a million dollars."

"Good," she retorted against his shoulder. "I'm worth at least twice that on a bad day."

"You are," Nick agreed fervently, his chin resting on top of his foster mom's rumpled gray hair. "You definitely are."

He thought about the conversation on the drive to the camp. By the time he'd started up the winding mountain road leading to Red Hawk Camp, he'd decided Ruby was mistaken—and not only about that nonsense about him breaking Cara's heart.

Cara might be going through a tough time, but she wasn't shaky. She was the same confident, bossy person she'd always been. He was sorry her marriage hadn't turned out well, but if anybody could handle raising triplets on her own, it was Cara.

She was doing a great job, too. Her boys were nice little kids. He'd had a lot of fun showing them how to skip rocks yesterday.

He'd detoured by the lake because he felt sorry for them. They were obviously miserable at camp, and that was worrying Cara. She'd helped him out, and he'd wanted to return the favor.

Maybe these three didn't seem too comfortable out of doors, but what little boy didn't like throwing rocks? Especially when those rocks were splashing into a sparkling blue lake on a sunny June morning.

He'd hoped to cheer them up, but he'd enjoyed it just as much as they had. When he'd skipped that first stone across the lake's smooth surface, three sad little freckled faces had lit up. You'd think they'd never seen a guy skip stones before.

Which, he'd realized, they probably hadn't.

So, he'd knelt down and given them an impromptu lesson. He'd loved every minute of it, and afterward, they'd thanked him over and over. So he'd hung around after taking them to the birds of prey show, let the little guy who got spooked about birds sit next to him. Told them a few stories.

It was fun.

And it proved Cara had this single-parenting thing under control. No big surprise there.

At the camp, he parked his truck and glanced at his watch. Time to head into the park ranger office and see what disasters he'd be dealing with today. Going by the past two days, there was no telling, so the sooner he got started, the better.

But maybe first, he'd stop by the dining hall. He'd check on Cara and make sure she had everything she needed.

As he neared the building, he sniffed appreciatively. Meat was on the menu, for sure, and something else, too. Something sweet. He picked up his pace.

When he walked in, Cara was checking something in the oven. Slices of ham sputtered on the griddle, making his stomach rumble hopefully.

"I don't know what all you're cooking, but it smells great."

"It's fried ham, scrambled eggs and apple muffins," she informed him without turning around. "That was what was on the menu. It looks like supplies are here for tomorrow's meals, but not the day after, so I'm guessing your cook—"

"Mrs. Lipscomb."

"Mrs. Lipscomb was planning to have more supplies delivered. If you'll give me her number, I can call and see what's been arranged and what I'll need to take care of myself."

"Sure." He pulled out his phone. "That's a great idea. I really appreciate you taking the job, by the way. Need any help this morning?"

Cara pushed the ham around with a long-handled fork. "Don't you have anything else to do?"

Well, yeah. There were probably half a dozen problems on his desk already. But they could stay there a little longer.

"Nothing that can't wait. It's the least I can do, seeing as how I'm the one who talked you into this." He offered her a smile. She didn't smile back.

"Tricked me into it, you mean."

"What are you talking about? I didn't trick you."

"You'd already convinced the boys to stay at camp before you offered me the job." She sent him a cool glance over her shoulder. "Hadn't you?"

He frowned. She sounded annoyed, and that didn't make sense.

"I thought you wanted the boys to come to camp."

"I did. I do."

"So I did you a favor."

"Because you wanted me to take this job."

"Because I was trying to help you out. Is that a problem?" He took a step toward her, then stopped. It might be better to keep a safe distance between them. She'd hit him with a spatula yesterday, and that fork she was holding looked very pointy.

"No problem at all. As long as you behave yourself from now on."

Behave himself?

"Look, Cara. I'm not one of your kids. And nobody's twisting your arm. Like I said, I really appreciate your help, but please don't feel like you have to take this job if you don't want to."

"I gave you my word I would." She began flipping ham slices over, one after another. "So I will. I just don't like being tricked. In the future, I'd appreciate honesty."

"I wasn't dishonest. Desperate, maybe. But not dishonest. I was trying to be nice. Your kids were miserable, and I felt sorry for them. I double-checked with you because I wasn't sure that the boys hating camp was the only reason you might not want this job. You don't exactly strike me as the wilderness camp type."

"I went to camp."

"Math camp doesn't count." From the look on her face, he'd scored a point. He hesitated.

He really was in a pinch, and clearly Cara could do this

job and do it well. But he didn't want her feeling he'd railroaded her, especially not after what Ruby had said this morning.

No, he had to do the right thing, whether he liked it or not.

"Look," he said. "I appreciate you fixing breakfast and being willing to keep your word. But maybe we'd better just forget about this."

Cara froze, a piece of ham poised in midair. "What?"

"You and I have never exactly seen eye to eye," he said. "So this was probably a bad idea anyway. No problem. We'll just scrap it and move on. If you don't mind handling breakfast and lunch today, I'll make sure I have somebody else ready to take over tomorrow. Okay?"

He had no idea how he was going to pull that off, but that wasn't her problem.

She didn't look at him. Very slowly, she placed the ham she'd speared back on the griddle. "Fine. If that's what you want."

It wasn't what he wanted at all, Nick thought irritably. What he wanted was for this camp cook problem to stay solved. And maybe for Cara to—just once in her life—*like* him.

But that obviously wasn't happening, and life had taught Nick to cut his losses.

"Okay, then, we'll call this settled. Now, if you don't need my help, you're right. I have other stuff to do. I'll check back with you before lunch."

He left the dining hall, allowing the screen door to slam shut behind him.

He stalked across the camp. And sure enough, back in his office, he discovered a mound of sticky notes, each representing some minor emergency. Now he'd have to add finding a new cook to the list, too. He sighed as the screech of brakes announced the arrival of the children.

He skipped breakfast and got started on his to-do list. Maybe he shouldn't have, maybe it was a little petty of him, but he did it anyway. He did bribe one of the counselors to bring him a plate, though. He was starving.

The fact that the food was delicious did nothing to improve his mood. He'd never find another cook as good as Cara. Maggie was the closest thing, but she was too busy with Angelo's to do much out here. Still, he'd play the I'm-your-brother card and ask for whatever help she could give.

He avoided the kitchen area all morning, busying himself with various odd jobs. He bumped into the triplets around eleven o'clock, and they wasted no time reminding him of his promise to take them out in the boat today.

"After lunch," he promised. As the boys left for a nature walk with their counselor, he checked his watch. He'd promised to drop by the kitchen in case Cara needed him to pitch in with lunch. She probably wouldn't accept his help even if she did need it, but he'd stop by anyway.

She wasn't the only one who could keep her word.

He braced himself as he walked into the dining hall. "Cara? Just checking in, like I promised. Do you need any—"

He stopped short. She wasn't here.

He scanned the empty room, silent except for the call of birds and distant shouts from the campers coming through the window screens. He walked over to read the menu posted on the refrigerator. Chicken salad, crackers and fruit. He opened the fridge to discover several bowls of prepared chicken salad inside, neatly covered with plastic wrap. A gigantic bowl of cut fruit was there, too.

He closed the door, feeling deflated. Cara must have taken him at his word. She'd prepared the lunch and left.

She'd kept her end of the bargain—mostly. That chicken salad looked like it would have been a time-consuming process, and the place was sparkling clean, so she must have worked hard all morning. Still, she could have let him know she wouldn't be here to serve lunch to the kids. What if he'd gotten busy and hadn't come back by?

But he had, so he could set out the plates and cups and get everything ready.

He walked toward the pantry to grab the crackers he'd seen stored there yesterday. Just as he started to open the door, he heard a funny, snuffling noise.

He froze and leaned closer to listen.

The kitchen wasn't empty after all. Somebody was in the pantry.

And that somebody was crying her heart out.

Chapter Four

Nick had pushed through plenty of dangerous doorways before. Nine times out of ten he hadn't known what waited on the other side, but he'd never wasted time worrying about that.

He almost always landed on his feet. He was good at sizing up situations and rolling with life's punches. And so, most of the time, while other men hesitated, Nick moved.

Most of the time. Not today.

He hesitated outside the closed door. Those muffled, miserable sounds had him caught in an uncomfortable web of indecision. If it was—as he strongly suspected—Cara sobbing in the camp pantry…well.

He wasn't the right guy for this job.

He was the only guy here, though, which gave him two choices. Open the door or walk away. And walking away from somebody in obvious pain?

That was something he'd never been good at.

He squared his shoulders, rapped on the door and opened it.

"Hey," he said. That was as far as he got.

Cara was huddled in the corner of the pantry, her arms folded on one of the rough-plank shelves, her head resting next to a jumbo jar of baking powder. At the sound of his voice, she straightened, swiping furiously at her face.

"What are you doing here?"

Nick didn't answer. He had no clue what he was doing

here. Every rational thought had packed up and left his brain.

Cara's eyes were attention-grabbing on an ordinary day—they were such an intense shade of green. But drenched with tears, and sparkling with wounded anger?

Eyes like that could take a man's breath away, turn his knees to jelly and make him want to tackle whoever or whatever had caused those tears in the first place.

In fact, they just had.

So he gaped at her for a second, as her expression shifted from indignation to irritation.

"Please, Nick. Go away and leave me alone," she said.

"Yeah. Sorry." He rubbed his jaw. "I don't think I can do that. Why don't you try telling me what's wrong? Maybe I can help."

Her brows drew together. "Nothing's wrong."

Nick made a skeptical noise. "Come on, Cara. You don't have to talk to me if you don't want to, but something's wrong."

Very wrong, going by the look on her face, a mixture of hurt, embarrassment and helplessness. He wouldn't have been happy to see that expression on any woman's face, but he really hated seeing it on Cara's. He didn't know why it bugged him so much.

But it did.

She seemed unsure how to answer, so Nick took advantage of her silence by pulling over a wooden step stool and sitting down.

"Might help to talk about it."

"It's personal," she said firmly.

That was his cue to back off. He recognized it, and normally, he'd have respected it.

Moving around like he did, he found himself weaving in and out of other people's stories, here today and gone tomorrow. Because of that, he always tried to leave a light footprint. He made it a policy not to get more involved in anybody's life than they wanted him to be. And when people told him to back off, he did.

Unless…

Unless it was one of his siblings. Or Ruby. Or someone hurting and ashamed who needed his help, whether they were willing to ask for it or not.

So he didn't budge.

"Personal," he repeated. He leaned casually back against the pantry shelves, feeling the cans of corn and tomatoes shift behind him. "That's usually code for *embarrassing*."

Cara rummaged in a pocket, producing a neatly folded tissue. He almost ruined the moment by laughing out loud. She was probably the only woman he knew who'd actually have a tissue when she needed one.

She dabbed at her reddened nose and avoided his gaze. "Sometimes personal just means personal, Nick."

"Sometimes," he agreed neutrally. "So, what'd you do? Goof up somehow?"

She stiffened and glared at him, and he lifted an eyebrow. He was right. She'd messed something up, and now she was beating herself up over it.

"Everybody makes mistakes sometimes, Cara." He tried a sassy grin. "Believe it or not, even me."

He was goading her, hoping that a taste of their old give-and-take would jolt her out of this mood. Instead her lips trembled.

"Mine are worse," she murmured.

"Unlikely. But okay. Challenge accepted," he said. "Let's compare notes. Is it as bad as forgetting to pack mosquito repellant on a mission trip in Belize? Did that."

"Nick—" Cara began irritably.

"Over seventy bites and I ended up in the hospital with malaria. Cost the nonprofit I was working with a ton of money." He'd paid back every penny, but since that didn't help his argument, he omitted that tidbit of information. "Your turn."

She studied him for a second. Then she lifted her chin. "My husband divorced me after I dropped out of college to put him through dental school to marry the secretary that I hired as my own replacement when I went out on maternity leave. Turns out, he'd been cheating on me with her for at least a year and a half by then, something I didn't notice because I was too busy taking care of our triplets who were born prematurely with some medical issues. According to Todd, the affair was my fault because I wasn't fun anymore. He has more money than I do, so he was able to hire a better lawyer, meaning I ended up with almost nothing. I had to move back in with my dad, who's a really sweet guy, but who isn't all that comfortable with little kids, so we're driving him nuts, and I feel really guilty about it. So, I'm pretty sure I win."

He saw the way she was bracing herself for his reaction, no doubt expecting the condescending sympathy people offered in situations like this. Somehow, he knew that would be the worst thing he could do, to humiliate her by feeling sorry for her.

So he took a different tack.

"Aaank." He made a buzzer sound and shook his head. "None of that counts."

Cara blinked. "What do you mean it doesn't count?"

"Those are your ex-husband's mistakes, not yours. And," he went on, "not even original ones. Come on. Cheating with his secretary?" Nick stretched his legs out across the pantry floor, crossing his boots at the ankle. "The guy's not just a jerk, he's a boring jerk. If you ask me, you're well rid of him."

"Easy for you to say." He detected a spark of the old Cara in the remark, and he considered that progress.

"Maybe," he conceded. "But would you really want him back? A guy like that?"

"No." The word was definite, but her lower lip wobbled. "Not that it matters. He's not interested in coming back. Todd never really wanted to be a father, so when the triplets came along he started spending all the time he could away from home. I've been a single parent right from the start." To his surprise, she kept talking.

Nick didn't stir, didn't move, barely breathed as the story poured out. Cara talking to him like this felt fragile, like when a butterfly landed on the brim of your hat. You had to be still and quiet if you wanted the moment to last.

So he stayed silent and just listened. Listening, he'd found, was an underused tactic for learning pretty much anything about anybody.

There was a downside. Sometimes you heard some pretty unpleasant stuff. More than once Nick had heard stories that had literally turned his stomach.

He listened silently as she described the humiliation, the financial issues, the anxiety of dealing with the triplets' medical problems all alone. The words poured out in a torrent, and she didn't seem to notice that he wasn't saying anything. He suspected she'd forgotten he was even in the room, so he kept his thoughts to himself.

That didn't mean he didn't have plenty of them. A guy who'd bail on his wife and three sick little babies?

Yeah. Nick definitely had some thoughts about a guy like that.

After almost ten minutes of talking—definitely a record for Cara, at least when it came to talking to him—she blinked and sputtered to a stop.

"I…" She stared at him, her face blank with shock. "I don't know why I told you all that." She sounded so horrified that he almost laughed.

Instead he answered seriously. "Because you knew I'd understand."

"How could you possibly understand? You've never been married." She paused and frowned. "Have you?"

"Nope. So I don't know much about marriages, maybe. But I do know a lot about do-overs." He rested his elbows on his knees. "I've been all over the world, Cara, and I've experienced a lot. Learned a lot. But I learned a couple of the most important lessons before I ever left home. One was that other people can really mess up your life with their mistakes."

"It wasn't just his mistake. I married him."

"Not the same caliber of goof, Cara." She'd always been too hard on herself. "But how would you know that? Until now you probably haven't had much experience dealing with mistakes. Yours or other people's. Side effect of being a perfectionist control freak, I guess."

The little jab worked. Her expression shifted from embarrassment back into the exasperation he was used to.

"Well, thanks."

"Wasn't a compliment." He offered a cheesy grin, and she rolled her eyes and sighed.

Yeah. They were back on familiar territory.

"Now, me?" Nick went on. "Other people's mistakes have given me grief more than once, and I've made plenty of my own, too. Little ones. Big ones." His grin widened. "Spectacular ones. And look at me. Still standing. Want me to tell you how to handle mistakes?"

She studied him. He waited her out, liking the expression on her face a lot better now. She didn't look hurt or embarrassed anymore. She looked skeptical—and a little amused.

"Why not?" she decided. "What's the Nick Marshall method for dealing with mistakes?"

"Float back up and keep going."

"Do what?"

"Float. Like a cork. Somebody or something pulls you

down, you don't stay there. As soon as you can, you bob back up to the surface. And then you keep going."

"You float and you keep going." She lifted one eyebrow. "That's it? That's your expert advice?"

He laughed. "You get what you pay for. And it works. Mostly."

"Mostly."

"That's right. Life's not a chemistry exam, Cara. It's not pass/fail."

"I certainly feel like a failure right now."

"Well, you're not. Besides, I know you. You won't stay down long. It's not in your nature. You'll figure this out and you're going to make a big success out of single parenting and teaching and all the rest of it because that's what you do. You make things work. Like breakfast yesterday morning. And speaking of that..."

He paused, trying to think how best to say this. "I should never have pushed you into taking on the camp cooking job. I didn't mean to trick you, exactly, but I did want to stack the deck as best I could, so you'd consider sticking around. I didn't understand how much you were already dealing with. The last thing you need right now is something like that on your plate."

"I wanted to do it."

She spoke so softly that he wasn't sure he'd heard her right. "What?"

Even in the not-so-great light of the pantry, he saw her cheeks flame. "The cooking. I wanted to do it. I just didn't like feeling manipulated."

Manipulated. By him. He flinched. Yeah, he could understand that, especially given what she'd been through with her husband. "Does that mean you want the job?"

She crossed her arms and shifted uncomfortably. "Don't feel sorry for me."

"Oh, for the love of—" He stopped and shook his head.

"I'm not feeling sorry for you. The camp needs a cook. If you'd like to step in and help us out, then sounds to me like we've got a deal. Do you want the job or not?"

She thought that over, Cara-style. A familiar dull roar thundered in the distance. He glanced at his watch. Almost lunchtime.

"Simple question, Cara," he prodded gently. "Yes, or no?"

"Yes," she said quietly. Almost shyly. "As long as we have…boundaries in place, I'd like the job. It'd be something to do. Something different. And I've always liked to cook. I think it might be…fun."

Fun. Nick tried to remember if he'd ever, in all those long-ago days when he and Cara had wrangled in high school, heard her talk about fun. He didn't think so. Cara and fun never seemed very compatible.

But fine. Whatever. The main thing was, they'd worked this mess out.

"Job's yours," he told her. "And it looks like you'd better hit the ground running." When she just looked at him, he nodded toward the dining hall where the roar was getting louder. "It's lunchtime."

"Oh!" Cara glanced at her own watch and gave a sharp exclamation. "I'd better get started!" She moved toward the door, then stopped.

She turned. He waited, but for once in her life, she seemed to be at a loss for words.

"What?"

The intensely green eyes met his, red-rimmed but resolute.

"Thank you, Nick," she said.

Then she pushed through the pantry door and out into the kitchen.

The next morning, Cara wiped down the last picnic table with brisk strokes. Then she stood back and surveyed her new domain.

The dining hall didn't look much different, but at least now she knew the wooden tables were clean. She lifted her head, sniffed and smiled with satisfaction. The cinnamon-sugar muffins smelled wonderful.

She checked her watch. Five more minutes. Then she'd take them out of the oven, put them on a rack to cool with the others and ladle more batter into the muffin tins. There were only two of those, so she was baking in batches. At least the oven's baking time was standard, so her early morning calculations were holding true.

She'd stayed up late reviewing the menus on the website, and she'd risen two hours early this morning, filling several notebook pages with strategies for managing the camp's upcoming meals and snacks. She was low on sleep, heavily caffeinated and happier than she could remember being in years.

She felt almost ashamed of her chipper mood because it made so little sense. This kitchen was a nightmare from a cook's point of view. Not only did it lack large cookie sheets and muffin tins, but it was full of splintery, hard-to-clean surfaces and the appliances were prehistoric. Worst of all, she'd surprised a blue-tailed lizard in the pantry this morning.

Or more accurately, he'd surprised her. He'd scurried up the wall and behind the canned goods while she'd screamed—and dropped the canister of flour she'd been returning to its shelf.

She'd held her breath while she'd cleaned up the mess and she hadn't stepped foot inside the pantry since without being armed with a broom, but she hadn't seen him again.

Not yet, anyway.

The other worrisome problem was Nick. She hadn't seen him yet this morning, and she was thankful. Part of the reason she'd stayed up so late working on the menus was because she knew the minute she settled down to sleep, her mind would start replaying yesterday's awful conversation.

She couldn't believe he'd caught her crying in the pantry. And not just crying, sobbing like a silly baby because she'd lost a job that she shouldn't have wanted in the first place.

Then, as if that wasn't embarrassing enough, for some reason she'd never understand, she'd unloaded her entire, humiliating story. On Nick, the guy who'd never missed an opportunity to embarrass her back in high school.

She didn't know what she'd been thinking.

But he'd actually been...nice about it. Really nice. She wasn't quite sure what to do with that. It was so...un-Nick-like.

"How's everything going?"

Nick walked through the screen doors as if he'd stepped right out of her thoughts. She was too stunned to answer, but that didn't seem to bother him. He sniffed and grinned. "Smells like it's going great."

"Ah." Cara struggled to marshal her thoughts. That wasn't usually too difficult a process, but with Nick smiling at her in his crisp uniform, hair still a little wet from his morning shower, it was proving surprisingly difficult.

"Fine," she managed after a second. "Everything's going fine."

"Need any help?"

Her heartbeat stuttered. Another morning of working alongside Nick? After everything she'd told him? That might be...uncomfortable. "I don't know—"

"Look." Nick held up his hands in a gesture of surrender. "You're feeling weird with me, Cara, I get it. We had a pretty intense conversation yesterday for two people who haven't seen each other in a really long time, and you're a private person. I'm not sure if it'll help, but you have my word that I won't be sharing anything you told me with anybody else."

That hadn't even occurred to her. Most of what she'd talked about was common knowledge in Cedar Ridge anyway, and while Nick had always had his faults—she'd actually made a list of them once when they were competing for a student council position—he'd never been the kind who carried tales.

The kind who would snap an unflattering picture of you and post it everywhere with a funny caption? Definitely. A gossip? No.

Some of her discomfort melted away. She appreciated that particular trait even more now than she had back in high school.

"Now that you mention it, I could use some help getting things set up," she said. "I mean, if you're offering."

He smiled. "Oh, I'm doing better than offering. I've already got it lined up. Maggie should be here in a few minutes."

"Maggie? Oh, so you're not…" Cara fumbled for the right words. Another curveball. She'd forgotten how regularly Nick tossed those her way. "Maggie's coming?"

"Just for a little while. She can't stay away from Angelo's too long, but you know how Maggie is." He smiled at her. "She's usually going in about ten directions at once, so she'll get plenty done while she's here. And she's a whiz with food."

"A whiz?" Maggie edged through the kitchen door, giving her foster brother a playful shove. "Surely I've passed whiz and graduated to ninja by now. Hi, Cara!" As she spoke, the red-haired woman shook out a crisp, green Angelo's apron and tied it around herself with practiced efficiency. "The cavalry's arrived. You shoo, Nick. You've got your own work to do, and since you're the stinker who talked both of us into this mess, we're likely to start throwing stuff at you if you stick around. Okay, Cara, you're the boss. Tell me what you need, and I'll get started."

"Thanks a million, Maggie!" Cara sensed Nick looking in her direction, but she kept her eyes strictly away from his. "Let me show you around the kitchen so you'll know where everything is."

She supposed she should thank him, too. It was nice of him to ask Maggie to come in. But somehow it irked her a little. Maybe he didn't really believe she could handle this job on her own.

Of course, after the way she'd fallen to pieces yesterday, who could blame him?

So, she busied herself showing Maggie around the kitchen and ignored him. Still, she knew the instant he'd left the camp kitchen. She sneaked a glance through the big, screened windows at his retreating back.

He certainly didn't seem perturbed by her snub. He was looking up at a songbird trilling in one of the trees, smiling as he listened. He looked relaxed and happy and… handsome.

Her stomach caught oddly, and for a second she didn't recognize the sensation. It had been so long since she'd felt it—not since she'd first met Todd.

She froze. She wasn't—she couldn't be—thinking about Nick Marshall like that. Of course not. That would be…

Ridiculous.

"Cara?" Maggie was watching her with a puzzled expression.

"I'm sorry," Cara said. "Did you say something?"

"Just that I think these muffins are ready to come out. Too bad I didn't know you were baking. I'd have trucked in some bigger pans so you could bake more at a time. But muffins weren't on the menu today, so—" She trailed off with a shrug.

"I know." Cara quickly removed the two tins from the oven. She and Maggie began transferring the muffins to a cooling rack. "I'm sorry. Today's breakfast was supposed to be oatmeal. I did make some." She gestured to the pot steaming on the stove. "But a lot of kids don't really like oatmeal, so I thought adding another option would be a good idea." She'd felt guilty about making that change, and she'd bought her own baking supplies in case someone objected to it. Thanks to her dad's generosity, she had a little more wiggle room in her budget these days, and muffin ingredients weren't expensive.

But Maggie only shrugged. "My own kids aren't huge oatmeal fans, so it makes sense to me. Mind if I give these a try? I didn't have time for breakfast."

"Sure. Help yourself," Cara murmured. She sensed a test coming.

She hoped she passed. Nick had liked her cooking, but Maggie baked for a living. Her standards would be a lot higher.

"Thanks." Maggie picked up a cooled muffin and deftly peeled off the paper cup. She took a big bite, and Cara held her breath, waiting for the verdict.

"This," Maggie said as soon as she could speak, "is excellent. Professional-level excellent. Muffins aren't as easy as most people think, so I'm impressed. Nick said you were an amazing cook, and he's right."

Cara fumbled clumsily with the ladle, dribbling a drop of batter on the rim of the tin she was filling. Her stomach was doing more strange little flips.

Because her cooking was being praised by a professional baker, she told herself firmly. The acrobatics in her midsection had nothing to do with Nick's compliment.

"Thanks. That means a lot, coming from you."

"Thank *you*." Maggie pinched off a bit of her muffin and squeezed it gently, checking the crumb. "What you're doing means a lot, too."

"Baking unauthorized muffins?"

The other woman smiled. "Helping us out. Nick only took this ranger job as a favor to Logan. We all thought it'd be an easy gig, but since the camp started up, he's been coping with one disaster after another. It's the first time he's been home for any length of time in years, and we hated for him to be run ragged the whole summer."

"Nick's been away from home for years?"

"Looks like you've got everything done." Maggie was whisking through the kitchen, scanning Cara's preparations with a practiced eye. "Not much I can do to help you, at least not today. But I can loan you some bigger pans and muffin tins so you can bake larger batches next time. Let me take a look at the upcoming menus and see what you're going to need." She frowned. "I thought Nick told me they'd be posted on the fridge?"

"I took them down." Cara rummaged in her tote bag and handed over the neatly printed sheets she'd revised on her computer. "I wanted to correlate them with shopping lists and figure up preparation times."

Maggie flipped through the pages. "What were we talking about? Oh, Nick and his wandering. To answer your question, he's been home maybe half a dozen times in the last five years. Not often enough to suit us, of course, and he never stays long. Nick the Nomad. That's what we call him. He flits from job to job, country to country. Every time we turn around he's created a whole new life for himself. Then just when we get used to that, he scraps it all and moves someplace else. He says life gets boring, otherwise. You've done a great job with these meal plans." She switched topics abruptly, giving Cara a speculative glance. "You're very organized."

"I like to be prepared."

"That's a good quality for a cook," Maggie said with a laugh. "Of course, so is being able to think on your feet. No matter how much prep you do, occasionally things just aren't going to work out the way you'd planned. How are you at that?"

Cara wasn't sure how to answer that question. Then she thought about her life, how she'd floundered since she'd found out about Todd's affair. "Not so great."

Maggie laughed again. "Well, it's a skill that can be learned. And you've got the best teacher ever right in front of you. Nick's the king of thinking on his feet. That's probably why he never bothers to do much planning—he's too good at last-minute saves. Between the two of you, you'll have this camp running like a top. I'll make a list of the baking equipment you'll need. Other than that, it looks like you've got everything under control. But if you ever find yourself in a pinch, give me a call. Like I said, you're doing us a big favor stepping in like this, so I'd like to give you all the help I can."

Maggie started listing the items Angelo's could loan the camp. Cara tried to listen, but her mind kept circling back to what Maggie had said about Nick. Nick the Nomad, who moved on when he got bored, who never stayed long in one place.

Then she remembered the silly way she'd felt when she'd seen him smiling up at that bird. And how her boys' whole attitude toward camp had changed just because Ranger Nick had taken a few minutes to show them how to skip stones on the lake.

The back of her neck prickled. She shivered and reached up to rub the feeling away.

"I'll get a piece of paper," Maggie was saying, rummaging through the drawers. "I should probably write this all down so we'll both remember."

"Good idea," Cara said, but she knew it wasn't necessary. She'd remember exactly what Maggie had said.

Every single word.

Chapter Five

"Lunch was great." Nick paired the compliment with a smile as he chunked his paper plate into the garbage. "Best sloppy joes I ever ate."

"Thanks." Cara offered a polite smile. "I'm putting the leftovers into the refrigerator. Would you let the staff know? Somebody should take them home and enjoy them."

Before he could answer, she walked away, carrying the big serving tin to the sink to wash. He lingered at the counter for an awkward second, then gave himself a mental shake and walked out the door.

He'd been trying to strike up a friendly conversation with Cara for the past week and a half, and he'd gotten nowhere. Ever since the morning he'd invited Maggie to come help out in the kitchen, he'd been getting the cold shoulder.

He'd been second-guessing that bright idea. Afterward, Maggie had assured him that Cara knew what she was doing and didn't need much help. And, his sister had added, women who enjoyed cooking tended to be territorial about their kitchens.

He should have minded his own business. But after he'd found Cara crying in the pantry, he'd wanted to do something—anything—to lighten her load.

The world was an unpredictable place. Personally, he'd always embraced that—enjoyed it, even, but there was no doubt life could take some nasty turns. He'd learned to be philosophical about that, and the faith he'd picked up in Ruby's little farmhouse helped.

But this bothered him. It didn't seem right for Cara Andrews, the hardworking, rule-following girl voted most likely to succeed at…well, everything, to be crying in a pantry because she'd fallen for the wrong guy.

So he'd tried to help. Maybe his idea hadn't worked out well, but sometimes that happened. He should shake it off and move on.

If he could figure out how.

He pulled a notepad out of his pocket, scrawled a note about the leftovers and stuck it on the bulletin board outside the dining hall. Then he followed the mulched trail leading away from the kitchen, trying to focus on the pleasant feel of the breeze and the fresh smell of the trees and the water.

He paused to watch a squirrel zigzag up a tree trunk, appreciating the nimble grace of the little animal. He'd rather be climbing a tree himself than heading to the office to return phone calls and deal with boring paperwork. It was a gorgeous early summer day, and after the snub from Cara, his mood needed a lift.

On impulse, he shifted direction, heading toward Bluejay Lake. He loved being near the water—he'd spent the better part of one year living on a houseboat in the Netherlands, and he'd found it incredibly peaceful.

Here, though, there wasn't much peace to be had. The counselors were giving the youngest kids a fishing lesson, and the grassy banks bordering the sparkling water buzzed with activity. Children were lined up at the edge of the water, miniature fishing rods in hand, all safely equipped with rubber weights, learning how to cast.

Nick leaned against a handy oak tree and watched. Easy to see that most of these kids had never held a fishing pole before. It was cute how excited they got when their line plopped into the water. None of them would win any points for form or distance, but they all seemed to be having a great time.

Well, almost all of them. He frowned, noting three little heads, clustered together. Cara's boys were having a lot of trouble mastering the cast.

Brian was the best at it, but even he couldn't quite manage. The other two boys weren't getting their rubber plugs into the water at all. As Nick watched, Aaron set his pole down and flopped on the ground, looking dejected.

Nick shaded his eyes. The adult counselor was on the far end, busy with a group of six kids. A few more campers were scattered along the bank, working independently and doing all right. The teenaged assistant counselor was on the nearer end of the line, helping another kid while three more pint-size campers tugged impatiently at his T-shirt.

Nick scratched at his jaw. Technically this was none of his business, and he didn't want to step on anybody's toes by butting in. The whole kitchen thing with Maggie and Cara had underlined how dumb a move that could be. Still, both counselors looked overwhelmed, and neither had noticed how discouraged Cara's sons were getting. After watching another five minutes, Nick came to a decision. He went to the teenaged counselor and pulled him aside.

"Hey," he said in a low voice. "When you get a minute, the triplets need a hand."

The boy looked frazzled. "They usually do. They have a hard time with anything requiring motor skills. Their mom sent a note about it on the first day. But I can't spend all my time with them. All these kids need help. You'd think none of them has ever even held a fishing pole before."

"Most of them don't have dads at home," Nick pointed out. "The triplets included. So you're probably right. Most likely they haven't ever gone fishing."

"Oh, yeah." The boy's cheeks mottled red. "No wonder, huh?"

"No wonder," Nick repeated. "Tell you what. I've got a minute or two. I'll go help them." He strode to the end of the line where Brian and Scott had joined Aaron on the grass, their poles discarded. They watched the other campers casting their lines, their expressions wistful.

"How's it going, guys?"

"Not good," Aaron said glumly.

"We stink at fishing." Scott had drawn his knees up to his chest and was resting his chin on his arms.

"I tried really hard." Brian looked the most upset. "And I listened when Mr. Chase was 'splaining, but I guess I didn't listen good 'cause I can't make it work." His lower lip trembled.

"It's okay." Nick tousled his hair. "Shake it off. Fishing's not something to get stressed out over. It's supposed to be fun."

"Not for us," Scott muttered.

"Here." Nick scooped up one of the stubby poles. "Let me show you how to do it."

He explained the mechanism of the reel as the little boys crowded around him. It took a while. Chase wasn't kidding about the fine motor skills. That was definitely an issue. But they really wanted to learn, and fifteen minutes later, he had them casting their lines into the lake.

Nick stood back, helping as needed, watching the boys master the simple skill. He glanced down the line of kids, wondering if he should offer to help anybody else. But as far as he could see, most of the others were managing all right, and the counselors were handling the few who were still struggling.

Anyway, the triplets were special. They were sweet kids, and now that he knew what they'd gone through in their short lives, he figured they deserved some extra attention.

"Uh-oh," Aaron said. His line was tangled in a bush on the edge of the bank. "I messed up!"

"You're snagged," Nick said. "No big deal. Reel in as far as you can and give it a tug."

Aaron complied, but the line didn't pull free. "Am I gonna get in trouble?" He sounded like he was about to cry.

"Nope. Tug it again. Hard," Nick said. He could go and untangle the line, but better if Aaron could get it loose by himself.

Nick had always learned best by figuring things out on his own. Those hard-won successes had taught him to have confidence in his own abilities—something he'd lacked early on.

These boys lacked that, too. Probably Cara had coddled them a little too much. Mothers did that sometimes. Well, not his. And definitely not Ruby. But he'd seen that tendency in other women, and in this case there hadn't been a father's influence to balance it out.

Unfortunately, the bush wasn't cooperating. Aaron's line stayed stubbornly stuck.

"I'm not strong enough, Ranger Nick." The child's voice quavered, and he swiped at his eyes. "I need help." And just like that, all Nick's big ideas about self-reliance and tough love went out the window.

Poor little guy.

"It's okay, buddy. Hang on." He started toward the bush to untangle the fishing line.

"Don't cry, Aaron. I'll help you!" Nick turned to see Brian grab the pole, positioning his hands around his brother's. Scott stepped up, too, and together the triplets gave the pole a mighty pull.

Nick smiled. Brotherly teamwork, he thought. Nothing like it.

He turned back toward the bush just in time to see the rubber plug pull free and sail through the air at high speed.

Straight at his face.

Alarm bells sounded a split second too late—right before the thing caught him in the eye.

"Ow!" He clapped a hand over his face. Whoo—that *hurt*!

A frantic chorus went up from the boys. "Mr. Chase! Mr. Adam! Come quick! We knocked Ranger Nick's eye out!"

"What?"

Nick could barely hear the counselors' panicked exclamations over a loud buzz of children's voices. He removed his hand from his eye to find himself surrounded by a blurry sea of bobbing heads.

"Be careful!" Scott yelled over the din. "You might step on his eyeball and squish it!"

A collective scream went up, and the sea of small people receded.

"Everybody calm down," Nick managed. He blinked, and the blurriness improved. He blinked again.

"Dude." Chase had reached him first. The teenager's face was pale. "You all right?"

"I'm fine."

"I didn't mean to!" Aaron was sobbing in earnest now.

"Not your fault, buddy," Nick assured him. "I should've ducked."

Adam, the adult counselor, looked into Nick's face and winced. "Better get the camp nurse to take a look at that. Eye injuries are nothing to mess around with."

"I don't think it's serious. I just need an ice pack," Nick said. "Probably just going to be a really impressive shiner."

"Want me to send a kid to the kitchen to grab you a bag of ice?" Adam asked. The kids immediately started up a new chorus.

"Me!"

"I'll go!"

"Me, me!"

"That's okay," Nick said. "I'll go myself."

Adam nodded. "Come on," he said to the campers.

"Ranger Nick's fine. Let's get back to our fishing lesson." The man began shepherding the herd of children back toward the lake.

Nick crouched until he was eye level with Aaron. "He's right, kiddo, I'm fine. And you guys did a great job of getting that line unstuck, too. You'll be champion fishermen in no time, all three of you."

"Can I go with you? To get the ice? Please?" Aaron asked, sniffling. "I wanna make sure you're okay."

"Mama's in the kitchen," Brian reassured his brother. "She'll take care of Ranger Nick's eye. She always knows what to do when somebody gets hurt."

"Yeah." Aaron swiped his nose with his shirtsleeve. "But I still wanna go with him. What if his eye falls out on the way? He'll need somebody to pick it up."

"My eye's not going anywhere," Nick said firmly. "But like I said, I could use some ice—and some company on the way back to the dining hall. How about you three walk me over there? Adam? You all right with that?"

"Sure," the counselor called back.

Even with one eye, Nick could see how the triplets perked up.

"We know the way, Ranger Nick." Brian offered his hand with an important air. "Don't you worry if you can't see so good. Us and Mama will take care of you."

"Thanks." Nick allowed himself to be led back along the path, the triplets crowding around him like overexcited puppies. He wondered what Cara would think when they showed up in her kitchen.

No telling. But hey, if she shot him another one of those chilly smiles, he might not need the ice pack after all.

"Seriously?" The teenaged counselor looked at the plastic container of sloppy joe leftovers in her hand. "I can take the whole thing?"

She'd stopped by, shyly clutching a note she'd taken off the camp bulletin board in scrawling black handwriting, offering camp leftovers to anybody who was interested. Nick had wasted no time posting the offer.

"You sure can." Cara had double-checked the rules in the staff handout she'd found. She could dispose of the leftovers in any way she chose—except that she couldn't feed them to the wildlife.

That was fine by her. She preferred to keep a nice, safe distance from all the creatures scurrying around the camp, thank you very much.

"Here." Cara plopped a baggie of leftover buns on top of the plastic lid. "You'll need these, too."

To Cara's surprise, the girl sniffled. "Thanks so much. This'll feed me and my brother and my mom for supper tonight." The girl swallowed. "My dad left last month, and we've been kind of struggling. My mom just got a new job, and things are getting better, but she doesn't get paid until next week, and—"

"Oh, honey." Cara gave the teen a warm side hug. "Believe me, I understand. Tell you what, I'll save all the leftovers for you from here on out, okay? What's your name so I can write it on the containers?"

"Livvie," the girl said softly.

"Got it." Cara nodded matter-of-factly. "I'm so glad we worked this out. I'd hate for the food to end up in the trash."

"Oh, no, you can't throw this away!" Livvie's brown eyes went wide with horror at the thought. "With you cooking, the food's the best it's ever been!"

Cara smiled. "That's really sweet of you to say."

"It's true! I worked here last year, and I know."

"Well, I'm glad you're enjoying the meals. Now, be sure to check the refrigerator before you go home every day. I'll label all the containers you're supposed to take with your name."

After the teenager left, Cara finished putting the kitchen to rights and tried to sort out her feelings. She hated that Livvie's family was going through a tough time. She could certainly empathize, and it felt really good to be able to help, even a little.

Since she'd started working at the camp, she felt happier than she had in a long time. She was touched to see how much everybody appreciated the simple meals she fixed. She'd learned that many of the teenaged counselors came from struggling families, just like the campers, and it warmed her heart to see them all enjoying plates of nutritious food.

She'd even secretly upped that nutrition here and there. For example, she'd pureed some cooked vegetables and added them into the sloppy joe mix today. Nobody had noticed, and it pleased her to know that the children had cheerfully consumed the additional vitamins with their burgers.

She felt like she was doing something worthwhile, and she was loving every minute of it. She had to keep reminding herself that this job was only for the summer. In the fall, she'd be teaching math at the college with her father.

Teaching was a nice, secure job. Not as much fun as cooking, in her opinion, but she was grateful to have the opportunity, and she planned to do her very best. If this job worked out, she could settle down here with her boys in a small house of their own, and hopefully give them a secure, happy life.

For some reason, her mind flitted to Nick. He certainly hadn't settled down. According to Maggie, he wandered from place to place as carefree as a bird, and he seemed happy enough.

She rinsed the rag she'd been using in hot water and wrung it out with a vicious twist. Then she threw it into her cleaning bucket with some force.

She didn't know why thinking about Nick's life irritated her. She should be grateful to him. Given their high school history, he was being far nicer to her than she would have expected. He'd given her this job that she loved, and he'd been going out of his way to be kind to her since she'd had her little breakdown in the pantry.

Nick Marshall being nice was a new experience. He'd never been mean, even back in high school. Just annoying. He'd delighted in teasing her, and the more self-controlled she tried to be, the harder he worked to startle her into doing something embarrassing or silly.

He'd been successful way too often.

Now, though, he was polite and supportive, always offering to help, even dragging his sister into the mix. Probably because he felt sorry for her, which, honestly, was kind of humiliating. And that sympathy, when coupled with Nick's charm, was also a little…confusing, so it was a good thing Maggie had shared those tidbits about her brother's lifestyle. Cara had needed the reminder not to get too attached, that this new, kinder Nick was only passing through Cedar Ridge on the way to his next big adventure.

Whatever that turned out to be.

She picked up the broom and began to sweep the floor with brisk strokes.

"Mama!"

Brian called urgently from somewhere outside, interrupting her thoughts. She turned, all her maternal instincts on full alert.

Something was wrong.

Dropping the broom, she ran across the kitchen and pushed open the screened door. For a second she couldn't make sense of what she was seeing.

She'd expected an injured child, but her boys were clustered around Nick leading him toward the dining hall. As she closed the distance between them, she noticed that Nick's right eye was fiery red and watering.

"What happened? Are you all right?"

"Yes," Nick answered.

"No!" her sons chorused at the same time. They all began jabbering at once.

She was used to interpreting overexcited triplets, so she gathered the basic information pretty quickly. Aaron had somehow managed to thump Nick directly in the eye.

"It was an accident," her son kept insisting tearfully.

"Let me see," she said.

"It's fine," Nick protested, waving a hand. "I just need an ice pack."

"Eye injuries can be serious," she told him. "You may need to go to the hospital. Let me see."

"Oh, for—" He cut off the exasperated expression and lowered his hand from his eye. "See? Nothing to worry about."

She leaned in close. She was only planning to look closely, to make sure there wasn't any bleeding or serious injury.

And there wasn't, not as far as she could tell. The right side of his face was red, but the eye itself looked fine. She squinted and moved a hair closer to make sure. Brown eyes looked into hers, full of impatient exasperation.

And—although it made absolutely no sense—for a second, her mind skipped off in an unexpected direction.

Nick smelled like the outdoors. Like sun-warmed clothing and fresh air and green growing things. And—faintly—of coffee, fishy lake water and sweat.

The smell of adventures—both good and bad—clung to this man like a cologne. Somebody should bottle that and sell it because she suddenly, inexplicably, wanted to do something...different. Something exciting and new, like the things Nick did all the time.

Which was silly. She blinked. The last thing—the very last thing—she needed in her life right now was an adventure.

She cleared her throat and moved back into a safer zone. "I don't see anything bad. I'll get you that ice pack."

She'd noticed several stored in the freezer, so she was back in a second with one, wrapped carefully in a clean dish towel.

"Thanks." He pressed it against his eye and winced.

"You should sit down, Ranger Nick." Aaron tugged on the ranger's free hand. "If you get hit on the head, sometimes you get dizzy and fall down. I seed it in cartoons."

"You've *seen* it," Cara corrected.

"Yes, ma'am." Aaron nodded earnestly, missing her point. "It happens a lot."

"He won't fall down," Scott assured his brother. "There's no stars spinning around his head. When they fall down on the cartoons, there's always stars."

Cara felt her lips curving into a smile. "Oh—" she started.

"Good to know," Nick interrupted solemnly. His uncovered eye twinkled at her, and the silly, adventure-hungry butterflies fluttering in Cara's stomach multiplied.

"Maybe he needs a drink of water," Aaron fretted. "Can I get him one, Mama?"

"Um. Sure," she said.

"I'll get it," Brian volunteered swiftly.

"I'm the tallest. I can reach the faucets the bestest." Scott was tallest—by half an inch. He raced toward the kitchen followed by his two brothers.

"I'm the one who almost knocked his eye out!" Aaron protested. "I should get the water!"

Nick chuckled, but Cara frowned as her sons squabbled in the kitchen. She should step in and settle the fuss, but instead she stood silently, as an ice block of worry settled in her chest.

Her boys cared about Nick. And not just a little. She knew her sons. They *really* cared about him—this charming, footloose guy who was just passing through all their lives.

This wasn't good.

"I could get used to this," Nick said, amusement rippling in his voice.

She looked at him, her forehead furrowed.

Nick frowned back. "What's the matter?"

"I—nothing." She walked toward the kitchen. "I'll get the water," she announced, taking the plastic cup out of Scott's hand. "You boys need to get back to your group."

This news was met by collective groans and protests.

"But Ranger Nick—" Aaron protested.

"Ranger Nick's fine. He's going to rest here in the dining hall and keep that ice pack on his eye while I walk you back over to the lake."

"I'd probably better get back, too—" Nick started, but she broke in.

"You rest right here," she repeated firmly. She shepherded the boys ahead of her, herding them toward the door. "Until I get back."

She was looking at her children, but out of the corner of her eye, she saw Nick shrug as if to say *fine*. He sank onto one of the benches, propping his elbow on the table so that it was easier to hold the ice pack in place. Obviously, he'd been through this kind of thing before.

That didn't surprise her a bit.

She walked the twins to the lake and turned them back over to their counselors. Then she retraced her steps, thinking hard about what she needed to say to Nick.

Because she definitely needed to say something—a very strongly worded something.

But polite, too. This wasn't his fault.

When she came back to the dining hall, Nick was lying flat on the bench, the ice pack over his eye. As the door slapped shut behind her, he opened his good eye and squinted at her without budging.

"Everything good?"

"I'm afraid not."

He straightened immediately, discarding the ice pack on the table. "What's going on?"

"The boys are really upset that you got hurt."

"Oh. Well, I'll hunt them down later and make sure they know I'm okay. Actually, it's kinda sweet that they're worried." Nick smiled, and she noticed the hint of a dimple on his cheek. Not a real dimple. Just the hint of one.

The man couldn't even commit to a dimple, for pity's sake.

"It may be sweet," she said. "But it's also concerning."

The suggestion of a dimple vanished. "Concerning? Why?"

"They're getting very attached to you."

Nick waited a beat. "And that's a problem because…?"

Did she really have to spell this out for him? Probably so. He wasn't a parent, and he'd likely never had a long-term attachment in his whole life. "They don't have a relationship with their dad, and they haven't connected with their grandfather. Not yet, anyway. I'd hoped with time… But now they seem to be glomming onto you."

"Glomming?" The dimple-hint flickered again.

"This isn't funny, Nick. There's a serious lack of male role models in their lives right now, so, of course, they're vulnerable. They're looking for a father figure."

"A father figure?" The amusement faded from Nick's face, taking the dimple with it.

"And the last thing they need," Cara went on, "is to attach to somebody and have him walk out of their lives." She tried to choose her next words carefully. "So, I need you to back off. It's nice of you to take an interest in them. I know it's because you feel sorry for me, but—"

"Whoa. Hold up a second, Cara."

"Please, Nick, let me finish."

She could tell by his expression that he didn't want to, but after a long second, he nodded. "Fine. Say what you need to say."

"I appreciate your compassion, but I don't want to see the boys hurt again, and you're only here for the summer, right?"

Another pause. "Right."

"So, please, just stop feeding their hero worship, okay? They talk about you at supper," she said in response to his quirked eyebrow. "It makes them feel special when you single them out. Which—" she went on doggedly "—is very kind of you. But given the circumstances, I feel it's..." She struggled for the right word. "Unwise." That one worked. "It's unwise to encourage them to form an attachment to somebody who's going to be leaving soon."

Nick stood and listened silently, eyebrows raised. Finally he said, "Are you done?"

"Yes."

"Good. My turn. First of all, I don't feel sorry for you, Cara. Do I hate what happened to you? Sure. You caught a rotten break, and I'm sorry about that. About *that*," he emphasized. "Not for you. Like I told you in the pantry that day, you're not the kind who rolls over and gives up. I never saw you back down from a challenge back in high school, and you're not backing down from this one, either. Everybody gets set back on their heels at least once or twice in their lives." One corner of his mouth tipped up. "Sometimes a lot more often than that. The people I feel sorry for are the ones who sit down when trouble comes, flap their hands and settle for whatever mess they're in. You won't.

It's not in your character. You'll get through this, and you'll be back on top of things before you know it. So, no. I'm not wasting my time feeling sorry for you."

Cara wasn't sure how to answer that. Strangely, it did make her feel better, so she nodded. "Well, thanks. I guess."

"As far as the boys go, that's a trickier question. They're not the only ones getting attached. I like them, too."

"It's not the same thing," Cara protested.

"Yeah," he countered. "It kinda is."

"But you're—" She trailed off, uncertain how to say what she was thinking without it sounding insulting.

"I'm not the kind who stays in one place very long."

She nodded, relieved. "Right."

"You think that means I don't get attached to people?" He laughed. "Of course I do. That's one of the best things about the life I lead. I meet lots of great people. Some stinkers, too," he added. "But mostly really great people. Sometimes I get involved in their lives pretty deeply. And yeah, it's only for a short while, usually. A few months. Maybe a year."

"And then you move on." He was making her point for her, wasn't he?

"I do. But not because I'm not attached, Cara. Because that's the way my life works. It's who I am. But that doesn't mean I throw away those friendships. I've stayed in touch with hundreds of people from all over the world. And you know what? I could show up at their house anytime and be offered a meal and a bed, no questions asked. Because we're still friends, good friends. Long-distance friendships take a little more effort, but they're worth it, so I do the work. And so do they."

"I just—I really don't want to see the boys get hurt," she whispered. "They've already been hurt so much..."

"They have, yeah. And they're going to get hurt again." He made the statement flatly. "That's life. Like I said, we all take our share of hard knocks, no matter how hard we try to sidestep them. You have to learn to trust God and keep going." He sighed. "I've done a lot of dangerous things in my time. Sports. Other stuff," he added vaguely. "One of the first things you learn if your instructor's worth their salt is how to fall, because you're going to do that. It's an accepted fact, and they teach you how to do it, so you don't get seriously hurt." He winked. "You might end up with a black eye or a bruise or two. But you'll be okay because you know how to protect the most important parts of your body. The most important parts of yourself. We're all gonna fall, Cara, sooner or later. Even the boys. You can't protect them from that forever."

Cara bit her lip, thinking hard. She hadn't done such a good job of that so far, in spite of all her preparations and plans. She'd been blindsided by Todd's infidelity, by his lack of interest in fatherhood. She wasn't sure how that could have been avoided, but there was no doubt she was no expert on protecting herself—or anybody else.

And she hadn't taken the fall all that well, either.

"Look," Nick was saying. "I don't know anything about parenting, but I've sure done my share of falling. I'm just saying maybe you should stop trying so hard to keep your boys from being hurt and start teaching them how to deal when life's not perfect." He held up his hands. "But, hey. This is your call. If you want me to back off, I will. Thanks for the ice pack."

"You're welcome," she murmured, but he was already out the door.

Chapter Six

Nick sent the email with the attached form he'd just filled out. Then he stretched and sighed.

Paperwork didn't have much to do with paper anymore, but it was still a pain. He looked out the window at the mountain scenery. The day was just as beautiful as when he'd been standing beside the lake watching the boys learning to cast, but for Nick the bloom had gone off it.

For one thing, he hated being stuck inside, and the view through the office windows wasn't helping. Being so close to trails, lakes and trees made sitting behind a desk even worse.

But his hatred of paperwork was only part of his problem. The rest had to do with his conversation with Cara.

He was usually pretty good at letting things roll off his back, but the barbs hidden in Cara's concerns had burrowed under his skin. She obviously didn't want him hanging out with her boys. He shouldn't have been so defensive about that, probably, but it had stung a little.

Okay, more than a little.

It had been a long time since the refrain of *you're not good enough* had repeated in the back of Nick's brain. It was in full force right now, though, and as loud as the chorus of frogs he heard when he drove up the mountain every morning.

He ran his hand through his hair, wincing as he brushed against his sore eye. It was puffing up, and he'd definitely have a shiner by tomorrow. He leaned back in his chair, hands clasped behind his head, closed his eyes and stretched his legs out under the desk.

What a day.

"You should keep ice on that eye."

He cracked open his good eye. Cara stood in the doorway, arms crossed in front of her apron.

"Yeah." He straightened in his chair and glanced at the ice pack she'd given him. It had thawed and was currently making a damp spot on his desk. "I probably should."

"There's no *probably*. I googled it after you left. You should put ice on it for fifteen minutes every hour today. Then tomorrow try warm compresses." She walked to the desk, picked up the mushy pack and made a face. "I'd better take this back to the kitchen and bring you a fresh one."

"You don't have to do that."

"My son caused the problem in the first place, so yes, I do." She hesitated. "About that. I've been thinking about what you said."

"It's okay." He wasn't in the mood for another lecture about why it wasn't a good idea for him to befriend her sons.

"Actually, you made some good points."

He lifted his eyebrows—and winced. Ouch.

"So did you," he admitted. "The last thing I'd ever want to do is hurt those boys. They're great kids."

"They are. And I know they're missing their dad. Well, not Todd, exactly. He was never very involved in their lives. More the idea of him, if that makes sense. It's partly why I moved back to Cedar Ridge. I'd hoped my father could fill that spot in their lives."

"But that's not working out."

"Not yet. My dad's a really kind man," she hurried to say. "He's just never been great with little kids. He does try," she said. "But, no. So far it's not happening." She twisted her hands together, looking uneasy. "And what you said, about learning how to fall, about how much richer your life is because of your friendships, even with people you can't see all that often… Well." She took a deep breath. "It's made me reconsider."

He had no idea where this was going, and he didn't want to mess things up worse than he already had. Probably best to ask his questions outright.

"What exactly are you reconsidering, Cara?"

She studied him, her eyes serious—and matching the tempting summery green shades outside his office window.

"Before I answer that, I have a question. Did you mean what you said? Do you really like spending time with my sons? Or were you just being…nice?"

He laughed. "When have I ever said something to you just to be nice?"

It was a rhetorical question—and a joke. But Cara-like, she took him seriously.

"In the past? Never. But lately…" She tilted her head. "Lately you've said several nice things to me. So I wondered."

There was no reason for him to feel goofy about that. But he did. And it made him irritable.

"Well, quit wondering. It's true. I like spending time with the boys."

She held his eyes for a second, then nodded, apparently satisfied. "All right. Then—if it's okay with you—I'd appreciate it if you'd keep doing what you're doing. Spend a little extra time with them, give them some attention. They really enjoy it." She sighed. "Like I said, you've been the primary topic of conversation around our supper table all week. You're their hero. The guy who can do anything, who's been to all kinds of interesting places, who tells the best stories."

"I'm flattered."

"You should be," Cara assured him. "They're not as

quick to warm up to people as some children, so it means a lot." Her expression clouded. "It also means that you could hurt them."

"I wouldn't do that, Cara."

"Not on purpose. But sometimes people like you don't realize—"

"People like me?" Nick broke in. "What's that supposed to mean?"

Cara answered without hesitation. "Confident people. People who don't care what others think of them. All the stuff that bounces off you can be pretty painful to the rest of us."

To the rest of us. Nick frowned.

Was she talking about herself? They'd sparred plenty in high school, but in Nick's memory, Cara had always given as good as she got. They'd traded insults and jabs like prize-fighters, and for his part, he'd enjoyed it.

Was she saying he'd hurt her? He started to ask, then changed his mind. For now, anyway—he'd stick to the topic at hand.

"I'll be careful of your boys, Cara," he promised. "As careful as I know how to be."

For the first time since she'd walked into the office, he detected a glint of amusement in her eye. "*Nick Marshall* and *careful* aren't words I'd usually put in the same sentence."

"Maybe not. But this time I'll make an exception. I give you my word." He shrugged. "If that helps."

It ought to. He made promises rarely, and he always kept them when he did. He knew what his word was worth, so it shouldn't matter to him if Cara did or not.

But he held his breath as he waited for her reply.

"It does help," she said finally. "Thank you, Nick, for understanding. It will mean a lot to the boys. I realize you have other things to do, so I'm not asking for any big commitment. Just please keep on doing what you've been doing and ignore what I said earlier."

"I'll be happy to do that." He paused, but he needed to make something clear. "For the summer."

He spoke casually, but when Cara's eyes met his, he knew she'd understood.

Their eyes held for a second too long. "For the summer," she repeated. Then she walked out the door, carrying the mushy ice pack with her.

Cara always followed through, so he'd expected her to return with a fresh ice pack. Instead, she sent it over with one of the assistant counselors.

"That black eye's going to be epic," the boy said admiringly.

Nick laughed and shook his head. It didn't take much to impress teenaged boys.

Or little kids. He couldn't get over the fact that Cara's triplets had—how has she put it? Glommed onto him.

He was still thinking about it later that evening at Ruby's kitchen table. His foster mom insisted he come over for supper a couple of nights a week.

"You ain't gonna live next door all summer and me hardly see you," she'd told him. "Before I know it, you'll be off to foreign parts again, and who knows when you'll be back this way? I plan on enjoying every minute with you I can get."

She hadn't had to twist his arm. For one thing, Ruby's cooking was something he often dreamed about when he was off in "foreign parts" as she called them. And for another…well. It was Ruby. Ruby mattered to him.

A lot.

Traveling the world had been an eye-opening experience. He'd learned some hard lessons. Met a lot of people, as he'd told Cara. Some pretty awful ones, sure. But plenty more whose kindness balanced the scales.

He'd always found the best people in the world's quietest, least notable places, not unlike this shabby farmhouse. Men and women who wore mended shirts and battered shoes, worked long hours, ate—and generously shared—small, unremarkable meals.

But these people—the ones who'd made the most lasting impressions on him—they hadn't lived small or unremarkable lives. Neither had Ruby. The world might say different, but he and his foster siblings knew better. In all his travels, he'd never met her match.

He knew he never would.

"What're you staring at me for?" Ruby asked him now.

Had he been staring? He supposed he had. "Sorry. It's not every night I get to have supper with a beautiful woman."

Ruby nudged around another chunk of the red potatoes she'd boiled and drizzled with butter. She ate less and less these days. "You got nobody to blame for that, but your own self. But that ain't it. What's on your mind, son?"

He started to say nothing. But to his surprise, he found himself telling her about his conversation with Cara. About the boys and how much he'd enjoyed them.

Ruby let him ramble without interruption, even spurring him on with well-placed murmurs of interest. When he'd finished, she chuckled.

"You act surprised that you're having so much fun with them boys."

"I'm more surprised they're having so much fun with me."

Ruby snorted. "Nothin' so surprising about that. You're the kind of man all little boys want to be." She shot him a teasing look. "Least until they get better sense."

"Cara seems worried they'll get too attached to me."

"I don't blame her. Her boys ain't got a daddy, and that

leaves a good-size hole for somebody to fill." Another sharp look. "You can understand that."

Yeah. He could. Ruby had done her best to fill that gap for him, and so had his mom. And he, Logan and his other brother, Ryder, had always been there for each other, too.

But still. Being a boy without a dad wasn't easy. "You're right. Since I'm only here for the summer, though, there's not much I can do."

"You can show 'em some kindness. And when the summer's over, leave as little hurt behind as you can."

He looked at her as he helped himself to another piece of roast. There was something funny in Ruby's voice just then—as if she wanted to say something but was holding herself back.

That wasn't like her. His foster mom never shied away from saying whatever needed to be said. "Okay, something's worrying you. What is it?"

She looked at him over her bifocals and set down her fork. "I wasn't sure if I needed to say anything, but since you're asking, I'm a smidge worried about Cara."

That got his attention. "Why?"

Affection mingled with the concern in Ruby's hazel eyes. "Well, because of the kind of fellow you are."

"What's that supposed to mean?"

"I didn't mean it bad." She swatted his arm. "You're a smart, handsome man with a kind heart. Young 'uns flock to you, and you're real interesting to talk to. I'm just thinking… A fellow like that might look pretty tempting to Cara Andrews right now."

Nick blinked. Remembering what his siblings had told him, he studied his mom's face for signs of matchmaking mischief. He saw nothing but worried lines grooving her forehead.

Relieved—and slightly insulted—he laughed.

"Trust me, you've got nothing to worry about. Cara would never be interested in a guy like me."

"And you know that how?"

"I just know."

Ruby lifted one gray eyebrow. "That ain't a real answer."

"This isn't a real question. It's ridiculous. Cara and I are as different as night and day."

"Well, when you've been through what that girl's been through, different might start looking pretty good."

He hadn't considered that. He frowned as he turned the idea over in his mind.

Then he suddenly remembered what his sister Torey had said when he'd teased her about the success of Ruby's matchmaking.

"It'll be my turn to laugh soon enough. You're up next."

He'd grinned. "I'm a confirmed bachelor. And forewarned is forearmed."

"I thought that, too, but she's getting sneakier," Torey had said. "She started off telling me how wrong Patrick and I were for each other. I was engaged before I knew it."

"You complaining?" her fiancé, Patrick Callahan, had asked, and Torey had smiled.

"Nope," she'd assured him, and the conversation had gotten sappy.

Now Nick gave his foster mom a stern look. "Are you trying some kind of reverse matchmaking psychology on me, Ruby? Because it won't work."

"Reverse what?" Ruby frowned back. "You mean 'cause of how things worked out with Torey and Patrick? That wasn't reverse anything. All I did was make sure they both knew what their lives would be like if they turned loose of each other. God did the rest. Besides, anybody could see they were made and meant for each other." She smiled. "Well, anybody but the two of them. But no." The smile faded.

"This ain't the same thing at all. Much as I'd like to see you married, I don't believe you're the right man for Cara."

Well, of course not. Neither did he. But somehow, hearing Ruby saying it was irritating.

"Why not?" he asked. When Ruby shot him a surprised look, he covered his slipup with a wink. "I mean, since I'm such a catch."

Ruby snorted. "Whether or not you're a catch depends on what a woman's fishin' for."

He spluttered a laugh. "I guess that's one way to put it."

"I ain't joking." Ruby got up and began gathering their dishes. He stood, too, doing his best to angle his way into all the heavier lifting. She didn't fight him on that as much as usual. She still didn't have her old energy back, and that worried him.

"You're a good boy, Nicky, and I love you with all my heart, but you ain't the settling-down kind. God gave you a wandering spirit. Now," she went on, twisting the faucet at the sink to let the water heat up for dishwashing, "I'll admit, I've fussed at the good Lord more'n once about that. I'd rather you settled down close by, like the rest of 'em, but you are what you are. You're gonna need a special woman to share your life, one who don't mind moving around and who's got the same heart for adventure you have. That's a tall order. I ain't found her yet, but I'm looking."

Ruby sounded so grimly determined that Nick didn't know whether to laugh again or be nervous. "Pretty sure I'm the one who's supposed to do the looking, Ruby."

"And you'd be looking, if you have the sense God gave a goose." Ruby plugged the sink and squirted in the dishwashing liquid. "But like I said, it ain't you I'm worried about. It's Cara. That poor girl's already fallen for the wrong man once. She sure don't need to do it again."

She lifted a glass to squint at it before giving it another

wipe with the dishrag. "Course, you're not a stinker like her ex-husband was, but you're all wrong for her, just the same. Cara ain't the sort who'd be happy living on a sailboat for months on end or spending half a year up in Alaska at a wilderness station with nothing but bears and other critters for miles around."

He'd done both those things and loved every minute.

"Hmm." He made a noncommittal sound as he stowed leftovers in the refrigerator.

Ruby was right, of course. Cara was a two-car-garage, good-school-district, weekly-schedule-on-the-refrigerator sort of person. And he…

Wasn't.

He knew that. Everybody knew that. So hearing it said out loud shouldn't bug him a bit.

But somehow, it did.

Cara kept an eye on the trail leading up to the dining hall as she scrambled eggs for Friday's camp breakfast. So far this was shaping up to be a nice day.

She had everything organized, the boys were loving camp and had adjusted to riding the bus. The kitchen smelled of fresh air, hot coffee and baking biscuits, and she hadn't seen that annoying lizard in the pantry all morning.

She added cream to the big bowl and whisked. If she'd timed it right, the first batch of biscuits should be ready when Nick stopped by for his morning visit. He could have one along with his first cup of coffee.

She smiled, then felt a guilty twinge.

The boys had asked if they could ride to camp with her this morning instead of waiting with her father for the bus. And she'd said no.

She'd kept her answer simple—only workers were supposed to be at the camp early. The boys had been disappointed. They were enjoying Nick's extra attention, and they'd hoped to ambush him today before the other kids arrived.

Nick probably wouldn't have minded. To her surprise, he seemed perfectly fine with being pestered by three pint-size boys. And there really wasn't any hard-and-fast guideline about bringing kids early. Nick's easygoing attitude was reflected in the whole camp, and any rule not related to safety could usually be bent.

But she'd told the boys no anyway.

She adored her sons, and ordinarily she loved spending time with them. But these mornings working in the bare-basics camp kitchen were precious to her. She'd secretly enjoyed having a few minutes to herself, knowing her boys were well cared for while she prepped the day's meals.

Of course, she wasn't always alone. Nick stopped by most mornings for an early cup of coffee. That had started after she'd backed off her request for him to keep his distance from the boys.

He'd caught her shooing the lizard out of the pantry with a broom, or trying to. The lizard was awfully quick, and it ran toward her as often as it ran away. She'd been two seconds from throwing down the broom and running for her car.

Nick had caught the lizard under a bowl and relocated him outside. Then he'd returned to help her catch up on the breakfast prep. He'd been back every morning since—officially for what he called varmint checks—because unfortunately the lizard hadn't *stayed* evicted. Nick generally lingered for fifteen or twenty minutes, even when there wasn't a stubborn reptile or an oversize spider to evict.

While the camp stirred to life outside the dining hall, they'd chat. He'd drain his coffee mug and taste-test anything she'd allow. Mostly it was just the two of them. The other counselors gathered in the assembly hall where there was a coffee pod selection and a variety of syrups and creamers.

Nick said he preferred his coffee plain—and that she brewed it at exactly the right strength. Which was silly, really, because she just followed the instructions. But still. It was nice to hear.

Anyway, she wanted to savor these mornings, because summer was slipping by. Last night, her dad had suggested it was time for her to start preparing lesson plans. He was right, but she wasn't looking forward to it.

Her father was convinced she'd excel as a teacher. Cara wasn't so sure, and when she thought about stepping into that classroom in September, her stomach clenched.

But how she felt didn't matter. She had to provide a stable life for her boys, so she'd simply have to do her best.

In the meantime, though, it was still summer, and she was determined to enjoy these pleasant mornings for as long as she could.

Nick showed up right on time, walking up the path, whistling a tune she was starting to recognize.

"Do I smell biscuits?" His deep voice carried, blown on a whiff of cool mountain air. "Hope one has my name on it."

"I'm just taking them out of the oven." She set the big bowl of eggs near the griddle and wiped her hands on a towel as he came through the door. "Ready for coffee?"

"I'll get it." He never expected her to wait on him when he came in like this, insisting she was too busy. "Want me to pour you a cup?"

"Thanks." The biscuits were perfectly browned. She carefully removed the huge baking sheet Maggie had loaned her, setting it on top of the stove. Nick paused on his way to the coffeemaker to whistle in admiration.

"Those are the prettiest biscuits I've ever seen. And I grew up in Ruby Sawyer's house, so that's saying something."

"Thanks." Nick never missed a chance to say something nice. She always tried not to show how much his praise pleased her, although she usually spent the drive home replaying the day's compliments in her head.

Not that they were anything so special. Nick was friendly to everybody. It had just been so long since anyone had complimented her that she…appreciated it more than most. These silly flutters she felt didn't mean a thing.

"Ouch." Nick had snatched a hot biscuit and was tossing it hand to hand to keep it from burning his fingers.

"Oh, for pity's sake!" She stuck a plate underneath his juggling act, and he dropped the biscuit on it. "Can't you wait five minutes?"

"I could." He blew on his fingers and grinned. "But the butter melts better when they're hot."

She laughed. "I guess you have a point. Go pour the coffee, and I'll get the butter out of the fridge."

"Eggs today?" Nick spoke from behind her, and she heard the gurgle of coffee going into a mug as she rummaged for the butter tub.

"That's right. Scrambled."

"The kids'll like that."

"I'm not so sure. They don't seem to love them, and they're on the menu three more times. Eggs aren't very good rewarmed, and there's always so much left over. It seems wasteful."

"Change the menus, then. Of course, that doesn't solve today's problem. Hang on a minute."

She turned around, butter tub in hand, to see Nick disappearing into the pantry, carrying his mug of coffee. He emerged cradling a jumbo jar of salsa against his chest. He thunked it down on the counter.

"Serve this with the eggs today. The kids'll love it."

"Salsa?"

"Sure. That's how my brothers and I always ate them."

"That salsa's for the tacos. On Thursday," she explained, because Nick was looking at her funny. "I can't use it up today if I'm going to need it later."

He continued to look at her silently, his expression growing odder by the minute. Was he insulted that she'd thrown out his idea?

Maybe she had been a little rude.

"It's not a bad suggestion," she went on, "The kids might enjoy doctoring their eggs up. I could set out grated cheese and chopped onions, too." The idea was taking shape. "Like a baked potato bar, only with eggs."

"Cara—" Nick spoke softly.

"But there's still the issue of the ingredients. I inventoried the pantry and refrigerator and cross-checked against the menus. Everything's already earmarked."

"Um. Cara—"

She waved a hand. "I know. I didn't have to do that, but I wanted to be sure everything was on hand. It's a long drive down the mountain for a missing ingredient. And—" She flushed, but she'd better be honest. "I can't afford to replace anything. I've done it before when I've deviated from the approved menu, but I'm on a strict budget, and—"

Nick set down his coffee and walked toward her, very slowly. She frowned as he approached.

"What—" she started.

"Look at me."

"Nick—"

"Just," he murmured, holding her eyes with his, "look at me, Cara. And don't move."

She started to ask what on earth he was doing, but somehow the words wouldn't come out. Instead, she just stared back at him silently.

He came closer, still moving slowly, his eyes fixed on

hers. She felt her heart stutter out of rhythm. Surely he wasn't going to…he couldn't be planning to…

Nick wasn't going to *kiss* her. Was he?

Involuntarily, her eyes dropped to his mouth. And the world exploded.

Nick reached out, lightning fast, just as a heavy, coiling weight fell on her right shoulder. She yelped, dropping the butter tub and sliding sideways across the front of the refrigerator. Her knees gave way just as her back hit the counter. She sagged to the floor, staring in horror at the glossy black snake writhing around Nick's arm.

"Oh my, oh, my, oh, my," she repeated helplessly.

"He's a beauty." Nick wasn't looking at her anymore. He was focused on the snake. He held it just behind its narrow head, as it thrashed and coiled its body around his arm. "Rat snake. They get a little aggressive sometimes when they're spooked, but they're harmless. He was perched on the refrigerator and got curious about you. He tried to take a sniff, lost his balance and slipped off." Nick chuckled. "Doofus."

Cara couldn't answer. She sat on the floor, breathing in short bursts.

A snake. A live snake had fallen right on her shoulder. She'd felt it, in that split second before Nick had snatched it off her. A heavy, moving, muscular *thing*.

She shuddered and closed her eyes. She really, really hated snakes.

"Hey."

She opened her eyes to find Nick studying her, his face concerned. "I promise he wasn't going to hurt you. Not on purpose. He might have struck at you if you'd scared him, but even that's unlikely. These are good snakes."

Good snakes. Ha.

"Could you—" The words came out as a croak. "Could you please take him outside?"

"Sure. Be right back. Don't throw away my biscuit." Whistling, Nick carried the still-twisting snake out the door.

Slowly, still shaking, Cara got to her feet. She walked to the screen door to make sure Nick took the awful thing far away.

"You and me both, honey." Angie, a wiry, sixty-something-year-old camp counselor, paused in front of the dining hall.

"What?" Cara blinked.

"There's something special about that one." She nodded at Nick's vanishing back, gave a dramatic sigh and fluttered her fingers against her camp T-shirt. "I'm old enough to be his mama, but he still makes my heart skip a beat. He's like one of those adventure movie heroes, isn't he? If I was young and unattached, I'd be staring, too."

Cara's cheeks started stinging. "Oh, I'm not… I don't—there was a snake—"

But Angie just laughed and waved as she went on her way.

Cara sank down onto a handy bench, hoping Angie wasn't a gossip. The last thing she needed was people thinking she had a crush on Nick.

Because she didn't. Did she? Her mind flashed back to the moment when she'd wondered if he was going to kiss her.

Didn't mean a thing, she told herself. A completely understandable—and silly—mistake. Pushing Nick out of her mind, she took some deep, calming breaths. By the time the buzzer went off for the next batch of biscuits, her knees were steady enough to go take them out of the oven.

Barely. And the large tray shook as she slid it onto the counter. But still, it was an improvement.

"You okay?" Nick came back through the door. He went to the sink and washed his hands.

"That depends. How far away did you take that thing?"

"A good distance." Nick paused. "He might show back

up, though. Snakes have their favorite hunting grounds. Sorry if I scared you with all that *don't move, look at me* stuff. I wasn't sure how you felt about snakes—"

"I don't like them. At all."

"Yeah." His mouth twitched, very slightly. "I'm getting that. Anyway, I was afraid if you panicked things might… uh…escalate. But honestly, he's not deadly."

"That," Cara said, "is debatable. He nearly gave me a heart attack." She considered Nick, who'd stooped to retrieve the butter container. "They really don't bother you? Snakes?"

"Nah." Nick poured out his cold coffee. "I've dealt with plenty of them. Some I worry about, but a guy like that doesn't make the list. Do you want to risk some caffeine or are you too jittery?"

"No coffee for me." Her heart was still hammering, but he seemed cool as a cucumber. Another timely reminder of how very different she and Nick were.

"I'm trading in my cold biscuit for a hot one," he announced. "That's my fee for snake removal."

"Worth it."

He shot her a thoughtful look as he slathered his steaming biscuit with butter and took a bite. "You sure you're okay? You're shaking. Here." Setting his breakfast down, he took her arm and led her to a table. "Sit. I'll get you some water."

He brought her a bottle of water and dropped beside her on the bench. "Everything's okay, Cara."

"Easy for you to say." She took a sip of water, embarrassed to see how the bottle trembled in her hand.

"Because it's true." To her astonishment, he crooked his finger under her chin, turning her face toward his. "There's nothing for you to worry about. If the snake comes back, I'll take him away again. If you use up the salsa, we'll buy more. If you don't like the menus, change them. And don't pay for anything else out of your own pocket, by the way."

She felt the curve of his finger under her chin, warm, solid, unyielding, his expression a mixture of sincerity and concern.

"Okay?" he prompted.

"Okay." She had no idea what she'd just agreed to. Angie was right, Cara thought dimly. There was something special about Nick.

"Try to have some fun. Freestyle with the food all you want. This is summer camp, not a gourmet restaurant." He winked. "If anybody complains, send 'em to me."

"Thanks." He had a biscuit crumb just southwest of his mouth. Without thinking, she reached to brush it away.

If she hadn't been so close, she might not have noticed the shift in his expression, the way his brown eyes widened slightly at her touch.

But she was, and she did. And for some reason it made her heart skip a beat.

She must not have been the only one who noticed… something…because Nick jumped up as if she'd pinched him.

"Look at the time. Kids'll be here any minute. You need help with breakfast?"

"Um. No." She swallowed and shook her head. "I can manage."

"Great. Okay. Well. I'll get to work, then. See you later, Cara."

He was out the door in five seconds flat, his half-eaten biscuit forgotten on the table.

Chapter Seven

That Saturday evening, Nick opened the refrigerator door at the Sawyer cabin and surveyed its interior. He was alone tonight—a rare occurrence—but his cupboard was most definitely not bare.

In fact, it was stuffed to the gills.

He pulled out a few containers and inspected their contents. All appetizing, all fresh, and he hadn't eaten since he'd had a quick sandwich up at the camp, but somehow the prospect of sitting at the table alone didn't appeal.

He stuck the food back in the fridge, stretched and sighed. The women in his family had filled the day with preparations for Torey's upcoming wedding, leaving the men in charge of the kids. Logan, Ryder and his brothers-in-law had invited him to hang with them tonight, but he hadn't had five minutes to himself since he'd come back to town, so he'd passed.

Now he wished he'd taken them up on the invite.

Which, honestly? Was kind of weird.

He'd been feeling off-kilter all day. He'd driven up to the park to do his normal Saturday checks, driven a four-wheeler around the trails, grudgingly put in some office time and taken one last pass around the deserted Red Hawk campground, making sure everything was in order.

He'd been doubly careful since it was Fourth of July weekend. The camp would be closed for an extra day on Monday, with the kids returning on Tuesday.

Everything had seemed fine. He'd picked up a stray candy wrapper or two, checked the doors, made sure the boats were secured. He was the only person there. While parts of the park were open to the public and would be busy on a holiday weekend, the camp area wasn't, and there was a locked gate at the bottom of the road that only staff members had keys to. All he'd heard was birdsong, frogs, and the occasional slap of a fish jumping in the lake.

That should have suited him fine. All his life he'd loved quiet places. Oh, he enjoyed hustling cities crammed with people, too, and the more interesting, the more offbeat, the better. But he restored himself in the silent, empty spaces of the world, and after the chaos of the week, he'd expected to find the empty camp restful.

Instead, he'd found it lonely.

He'd lingered in the dining hall. In typical Cara fashion, it had been neatly prepped. Fresh towels were hung on hooks, and all the cooking utensils were neatly stowed away.

A notepad rested on the scrubbed counter. He'd paused to read Cara's to-do list. Cut fruit, check on flour supplies. Get more salsa.

The last entry read *Create new menus?*

That question mark bugged him. Why shouldn't Cara change the menus if she wanted to? Nobody would care—and if they did, he'd deal with it.

But the question mark—that told him she still wasn't sure it was okay to trust her own instincts.

Or his.

He couldn't blame her. He wasn't so sure he trusted himself, either, not since that moment when Cara had innocently brushed her hand across his face.

He didn't know exactly what had happened, but for one

inexplicable second he'd come awfully close to doing something really…

Foolish.

Restless, Nick walked across the living room to the cabin's front windows. The scenery here wasn't as spectacular as the views at the camp, but still beautiful, slopes lush with trees, green leaves rippling in the early evening breezes.

That view wouldn't change for a while. It was June, and this was Georgia, where summer stretched out well past August, where the first freeze often didn't happen until late October.

If then.

Summer had only just settled in, and her stay would be long. By the time those leaves shifted into golds and reds, he wouldn't be here. He planned to leave a day or so after Torey's August wedding. Where he'd be going was more of a question. There were half a dozen interesting possibilities in his inbox already. There always were.

That's what he'd do this evening, he decided. He'd scroll through the emails and narrow down the possibilities for his next adventure. He should've done that already. He wasn't sure why he hadn't.

Tonight he would. Apparently he needed the reminder that he was only here temporarily.

A sparkle of headlights off to the right caught his eye. They vanished, then flashed again. He lifted an eyebrow. Somebody was inching up the mountain, heading for the cabin, and he wasn't expecting company.

He walked out onto the porch and waited. The shadows from the trees had grown long and lazy, proof the afternoon was nearly spent. Back when he lived here in Cedar Ridge, the length of those shadows had been his signal to leave the woods and head back to Ruby's for supper. His lips curved at the memory.

There was something comforting about knowing a place so well that the fall of the shadows told you the time of day, that the scent in the air warned you of the weather. Like right now… He squinted at the sky. A thunderstorm was coming. He could smell it.

This was the only place he'd ever stayed long enough to learn things like that.

When a white minivan pulled into the driveway, Nick's eyebrows went up another notch. What was Cara doing all the way up here? He went down the steps two at a time and strode across the yard to meet her.

Cara pushed open the door and stepped out. For once, she didn't look perfectly put together. Her hair was pulled up into what his sisters called a "messy bun," lopsided and loose, with bits escaping to frame her face. She wore a casual, flowered dress made of some kind of T-shirt material and flip-flops.

She waited for him by the van, which, he noticed, was still running. She was twisting her hands together and biting her lip. She looked uncertain—and flustered, and the hopeful expression in her eyes made his stomach flip over.

Stop it, he told himself sternly.

"I wasn't sure you'd be home," she said when he came within earshot. "I should've called first, but I just… I'm sorry. Is this a good time?"

"A good time for what?" he asked. "Is something wrong?" Making unscheduled visits was a very un-Cara-like thing to do.

"Not wrong exactly. I just…needed to talk to you."

Uh-oh. His mind flashed guiltily back to that crazy moment in the camp dining hall. Cara had always been scary smart. Had she guessed that for one split second he'd imagined closing the gap between them and kissing her?

Hopefully not. Because that would be…a problem.

"Okay." He braced himself but she didn't say anything else. "Want to talk inside? Or on the porch? Or—?"

She thought that over. "Inside would be easiest."

"All right." He motioned toward the house, but she didn't budge. Her cheeks went slightly pinker.

"I brought some things," she said. "I'll need help carrying them in."

He was officially confused now. "Sure."

She reached inside the van and turned off the engine, then popped the hatch. He walked around to the back. "The cooler?"

"It's full of food," she explained. "And padded with towels to keep everything hot during the drive. It took both my dad and me to get it into the car."

"Okay." He waited, but she didn't offer any further explanation. She just looked at him with that pucker between her eyebrows, worrying her bottom lip with her teeth.

He started to ask the questions that were multiplying like rabbits in his mind. Then he thought better of it.

He was on thin ice right now. Better just let this roll and see where they ended up. Cara would tell him why she was here sooner or later. In the meantime, he'd play along and hope for the best.

He took hold of the handles on either side of the cooler and tested the weight. Not too bad.

"I can carry this alone," he decided. "If you don't mind opening the cabin door."

Once inside the cabin, he set the cooler in the kitchen. Cara lingered in the cabin's living room, looking around.

He gave it a quick once-over himself, and relaxed. He wasn't a clean freak, but he tended to keep his living areas decent. Partly because he didn't own enough junk to spread over a large area. And partly because, while dirt didn't scare him, he preferred his personal space to be sanitary.

Cara caught him watching her. She tucked a tendril of hair behind her ear and offered an apologetic smile.

"I've never been up here before," she said. "My dad came once, with a school group. He says this cabin's a state treasure. He believes it should be turned into a historical site."

"Maybe it will be when Ruby's gone." Nick didn't like saying that—or even thinking it, but thoughts like that had been creeping around the edges of his mind ever since he'd come home.

Ruby had aged since his last visit. It wasn't just the new wrinkles or the lack of energy, or the way she pushed food around on her plate. Last night at supper, she hadn't been nearly as excited about this day of wedding preparations as he'd have expected.

He was worried about her. They all were.

Time to change the subject. "So? Now that you've seen it, what do you think?" he asked.

"It's very nice," Cara responded politely.

"Nice." He made a face. "Be honest. Not your kind of place?"

No, a cabin like this definitely wouldn't be Cara's pick. She'd probably prefer a prim Victorian. With fussy shutters and a perfectly kept lawn mowed by a husband with a steady, predictable office job.

Cara looked surprised to be put on the spot, but she took the bait. "It's just surprising," she said. "You'd think this much wood would make a space feel—" She seemed to search for a word. "Dark. Small. This place doesn't have that feel at all." She laid a palm against the solid walls. "It feels cozy. Strong and safe. I like it. But it really doesn't seem much like you."

He stared for a second, then laughed.

She realized what she'd said, and her face went red. "I'm sorry. I didn't mean—"

"No offense taken." He was curious, though. He looked around the room. A small leather couch and a recliner. Rag rug, bright with color. Big, river rock fireplace. One of Ruby's afghans tossed over the arm of a rocking chair. He liked it well enough. In fact, it suited him a lot better than most places. "What did you expect?"

"I don't know exactly. It's just… You've lived such an interesting life. I'd expected to see… I don't know…souvenirs I guess, from all your travels."

For a second, he didn't answer. The shy admiration in her voice had surprised him.

Cara Andrews admired him? That was…unexpected. And for some reason, it brought up the memory of that dining hall moment again.

To cover his confusion, he focused on unfastening the latch on the cooler. "I'm only here for the summer," he reminded her. "And I don't really collect souvenirs."

He heard the soft sound of her steps as she walked toward the kitchen, but he was careful not to look over his shoulder.

"I don't think I could do that. Visit interesting places and not bring anything home with me."

"I don't have a permanent address where I can store things. Besides, I didn't say I never bring anything back. I bring back memories. Photos. Friendships. New skills I've picked up. Stuff that doesn't take up space. Okay if I open this?" He levered up one corner of the cooler lid, waiting.

"Go ahead." Cara drew a deep breath.

As he lifted the lid, she stepped forward to remove a thick pink towel. Underneath were neatly stacked containers of food. A mingle of delicious smells drifted up.

"What's all this?" Nick picked up one of the containers. It was warm.

"That one? Fish tacos." Cara took it out of his hand and

set it on the table. "And this..." She reached back into the cooler. "This is pineapple chicken kebabs, and this one is barbecue chicken quesadillas. And this is my attempt at apple-sausage breakfast sandwiches. I tried them two ways."

She stacked the containers on the table and began cracking them open, one by one. "First with biscuits, but they were too crumbly, although they tasted good. So then I tried them with English muffins. I think that works better, but I brought both versions. I also brought some banana bread pancakes. I'm not sure how well they'd transport, and I didn't bring syrup because honestly, I don't think they need them. But butter would be good. Do you have butter?"

He stared at her. "I have no idea. Probably." Okay. He was going to have to come right out and ask. "Cara, what's all this about?"

She glanced at him and frowned. Wasn't it obvious?

"I need you to approve my new menus. I brought a list." She burrowed in her purse and pulled out a folded piece of paper and a pen. "I'll mark the recipes that you're okay with." She nudged the container with the fish taco closer. "Try that one first."

"What do you mean *approve* them?"

"For the camp," she said, unsure why he wasn't getting this.

Of course, in fairness, she'd shown up on his doorstep with ten different dishes for him to taste-test without even checking first to make sure it was all right.

She'd just been so excited about these recipes, and deep down, she'd been afraid if she'd called and asked permission to come, he might have said no. She'd hardly seen Nick since he'd abandoned his biscuit yesterday morning, and when they'd bumped into each other at camp, he'd acted uncomfortable.

She blamed herself. She'd somehow made things weird between them, and she hated that. She really didn't want to lose their new friendship, and she sensed that the longer they went without talking, the more awkward things would get. It was a holiday weekend, too, which meant an extra day off on Monday for the Fourth of July.

She didn't want to stew over this until Tuesday.

So she'd come up with this idea while cooking test batches of the most promising recipes she'd found. She really didn't feel comfortable making sweeping changes without somebody in charge signing off on it. Nick couldn't know if the food was all right if he didn't try it, and it wouldn't be half so good warmed up later. Much better to taste all the options while they were fresh.

So, she'd decided to do just what Nick had suggested back at the camp.

Freestyle a little.

It had seemed like a good idea in the safety of her dad's kitchen, but her confidence had flagged on the drive over. Maybe Nick wasn't home or was busy with his family or had already eaten.

But in spite of her lack of planning, things had worked out after all.

Or would, maybe, if he'd actually taste the food.

"I'm sorry to spring this on you with no warning," she said, her pencil hovering over the yes column on her paper. "But since I'm already here, why don't we go ahead and get this done?"

Nick lifted his eyebrows and considered her. "Okay." He picked up the taco.

Cara kept her pencil poised, reading Nick's expression.

Oh, yes. He definitely liked it. Her mouth tipped up with satisfaction.

"All right?" she inquired briskly.

"Better than all right. Amazing." He took another bite as Cara put a triumphant check on the paper. Then she took the taco out of his hand.

"Hey! I wasn't done with that."

Cara's smile widened as she plopped the half-eaten taco back into its container. That sounded like the old Nick. Just as she'd hoped, this plan of hers was bridging the gap between them.

"You can't fill up. You have lots of other dishes to try. Here." She moved a pineapple chicken kebab onto his plate. "This recipe calls for grilled chicken, but that can be done ahead, and the chicken reheated in the oven to make the prep quicker. And while fresh pineapple would be ideal, the canned chunks will work and be less expensive."

Nick picked up the kebab and inspected it with interest. He stuck the end of it in his mouth to slide off a chunk of grilled chicken, pineapple and bell pepper. Cara frowned.

"I'm crossing those off the list," she decided.

"What?" Nick said as soon as he could speak. "Why? They're delicious."

"They're also dangerous. I don't know what I was thinking. Little kids? Food on skewers?" She shook her head. "Not a good idea."

Nick examined the half-eaten kebab again. "You're probably right. I wouldn't have thought of that."

"Yes, well, you're not a parent," Cara pointed out. "Once you have kids, you start thinking differently. You see danger everywhere." She took the kebab out of his hand and scooted a breakfast sandwich onto his plate. "Well," she amended. "Maybe not you. You've never been scared of anything."

"I don't know. Being responsible for newborn triplets might have scared me some. Three babies at once is a lot. That must have been a crash course in parenting for you and your husband."

"Mostly for me." Cara spoke absently. She was trying to figure out how she could restructure the kebabs into a more child-friendly dish. "Todd wasn't very involved."

"His loss."

She looked up, startled at his tone. He sounded almost… angry.

"It was a loss for everybody," she agreed softly. "The triplets really needed both parents."

"I'm sure you needed a husband, too. Didn't you?"

She had, yes. Desperately. Even now, whenever she remembered those days, her heart sped up with leftover anxiety. It would have been different if she'd had a mother to help, but she hadn't. Todd's parents were divorced, and he and his mom weren't on speaking terms, so she'd had no help from that quarter.

She didn't want to share those details with Nick, so she shrugged. "I managed." Barely. And not always so well. But she had.

"You sure did." That was all he said, but the approval in his voice made a confusing warmth stir in her stomach.

She'd better steer this conversation to safer ground.

"Try the breakfast sandwich."

"I will." But he made no move to do it. "I'll taste everything, but you don't have to clear every dish with me. Cook whatever you want. Just stick within a reasonable budget, try to use up as many of the supplies that are already stocked as you can, and update the menus on the website so the kids and the parents know what's being served."

She blinked. Whatever she wanted. She wasn't sure what to say, except… "Well, thank you."

"You can thank me by giving me back my taco." When she scooted the container in his direction, he picked it up and took another bite, making an appreciative noise. "You know," he said when he could speak, "you're an incredible cook. Too bad you love math so much."

"I don't love math." The words popped out before she could stop them.

"What?"

"I'm good at math. There's a difference."

Nick chewed thoughtfully. "Most people love what they're good at."

"Not always." She shrugged. "You're great with kids, but like you said, you wouldn't want to take on a set of triplets."

She was trying to lighten the mood, but something flickered in his eyes. He shook his head.

"That's not what I said. I said it might have scared me. I didn't say I wouldn't have wanted to do it."

She had the feeling she'd insulted him. She hadn't meant to, and she hurried to make amends.

"Well, I'm sure you'd have done a great job. My boys certainly enjoy spending time with you. In fact, they're plotting to wrangle more fishing lessons. They're still having some trouble with their casting. I told them you probably wouldn't have time, but—"

"I'll make the time. It's no problem. Just bring them in extra early one morning. You know, so they don't miss out on any of the other activities, and so the other kids don't horn in."

"That's kind of you, but I don't want them to be an imposition."

Nick made an impatient noise. "They won't be. I enjoy spending time with them. Why don't we plan on it for Tuesday morning, weather permitting. Okay?"

"Okay. Thank you."

"Nobody has to thank me for spending an extra hour fishing. You love cooking, I love fishing. Even did it professionally for a while. Have you ever considered cooking as a career?"

He wasn't going to leave this alone. She laughed uncomfortably. "I already have a career. Or I will come September."

"Doing what? Teaching? You don't seem nearly as enthusiastic about that."

"That doesn't matter." She was probably wasting her breath explaining this to a guy like Nick, but she'd give it a try. "I'm a single parent responsible for three boys. I need a stable, steady job with good benefits and regular hours. Cooking is just a fun hobby."

"If cooking is what you love and what you're good at," Nick countered, "it should be more than a hobby. As far as being responsible for your boys, there's more to that than showing them how to earn a steady income and balance their bank accounts. Don't you want to show them how to enjoy their lives?"

"Of course. But—"

"If I had kids, I'd want them to see me using the gifts God gave me. I mean, sure. You balance that with common sense. But if you never do what you're gifted to do, what kind of example are you setting? Don't you want more out of life, Cara? Not just for them, but for yourself? Because if you don't, you should."

He spoke passionately, his brown eyes intense on hers. She stared back at him helplessly. In a dim corner of her mind she wondered how on earth they'd gotten onto this topic—and why it was that whenever she was around this man she felt like the ground was slipping out from under her feet.

She was tired of that feeling. She'd come out here to

patch up their friendship, and here they were in the middle of another touchy conversation.

"Why do you even *care* what I do?" she demanded in a desperate whisper.

"I don't know," he answered. "I just do. You light up when you talk about cooking, but when the subject of teaching comes up, all that sparkle drains away. It makes me… mad. I know parenting requires some sacrifices, but you deserve to be happy, too, Cara."

She swallowed hard. He meant to be nice. She knew that. But his words sounded unpleasantly familiar.

Todd had often complained after the triplets were born that he deserved to be happy—and that she was keeping him from it. He didn't want to stay home and take a turn with the boys. He wanted to play racquetball or hang out with his friends.

It had been hard for her to sympathize when she was so worried and sleep deprived that even a trip to the grocery store seemed daunting.

She wasn't fun anymore, he'd complained. She was always exhausted, always worried, always busy. Always asking him to do something he didn't want to do.

Nick and Todd seemed like very different men, but maybe they were more alike than she'd thought.

She suddenly felt very tired.

"You know what? I should go. I've already taken up too much of your time. You can finish tasting these and let me know if there's anything that you don't like. Just bring the cooler back with you to camp on Tuesday."

"Wait, Cara." Nick ran a hand through his hair, a pained expression on his face. "Look, I'm sorry. I don't know why I keep butting into your business. You're right. It's not… I shouldn't care so much. I have absolutely no right to have opinions about your personal life."

"No, it's fine." She waved a hand, trying for casual. "You're entitled to your opinions. We're just…different people. That's all. We always have been."

He was watching her closely, his face troubled. "I guess so. But—"

"I'm sorry, but I've really got to go. It's not fair to ask my dad to babysit for too long." Before he could say anything else, she was at the door. She forced a smile. "See you at camp on Tuesday!"

"Come early so I can take the boys for that fishing lesson. But, Cara, seriously—"

"Great! We'll see you then!" While he was still speaking, she hurried down the steps and across the yard. By the time she'd started the van, he was halfway across the yard, and he motioned to her to roll down her window.

She waved briskly, as if she'd misunderstood the gesture, and a few seconds later, she was bumping down the narrow mountain road toward the highway.

Chapter Eight

On Tuesday morning, Cara smoothed Aaron's hair, and stood back to give the triplets a final check. "Let me look at you."

Her boys sure didn't look as neat and tidy as they had the first few days of camp. Their Camp Red Hawk T-shirts were already slightly faded. Their new tennis shoes were grubby, and their socks—once sparkling white—weren't sparkling anymore. Georgia red mud was hard to get out.

But while their socks might not be sparkling, their eyes certainly were. They were excited to be returning to camp. She'd taken them to the Cedar Ridge Fourth of July parade yesterday, and they'd had the traditional hamburgers and watermelon lunch. None of that had compared to this.

"We gotta hurry, Mama," Brian said. "Ranger Nick's teaching us to fish today, 'member?"

She remembered, all right. And if she hadn't, Nick had texted her last night reminding her.

"Just us," Scott added importantly. Three pairs of green eyes looked at her, bright with eagerness, and the little boys bounced up and down on their smudged shoes as they waited for her go-ahead.

"All right. Get your water bottles and your backpacks and I'll meet you at the van."

The boys cheered and stampeded to do what she'd asked. She laughed and turned to put the brush away.

She found her father eyeing her from the kitchen doorway, his cup of coffee steaming in his hand. "Going in early?"

"Yes, and I'm taking the boys with me." She hurriedly gathered up her purse and tote bag. "They have an extra fishing lesson scheduled."

A lesson she might have skipped, given how she and Nick had left things on Saturday. She wasn't particularly looking forward to facing him this morning, but the boys were excited, and that was what mattered. "What did you think about the banana bread pancakes?"

"Delicious, like everything else you make. You're a very competent cook." He spoke absently, flipping through the stack of mail she'd placed on the end table.

Competent. "Thanks, Dad." She paused halfway to the door and glanced back at him. "I'm really enjoying cooking at the camp."

Her father made a noncommittal noise. "You always did like cooking, which was a good thing, I suppose." He shook his head ruefully. "None of the housekeepers I hired after your mother died were very proficient in the kitchen, and I barely know one end of a spoon from the other."

He was frowning now, his forehead creased with worry. Her father had always fretted over her lack of a mother, always worried that he hadn't managed well as a single parent. In some ways, his concerns were valid. His scholarly personality wasn't a perfect fit for single fatherhood, but he'd done his best. Now a single parent herself, Cara appreciated that more than ever.

"I didn't mind." She took a breath. "In fact, lately I've wondered if maybe my love for cooking could be…more than a hobby."

Her father's face went blank with astonishment. He shook his head. "No need for that. You have a very desirable teaching position lined up at the college."

A position he'd gone to considerable trouble to get for her. She felt a flush of guilt, but somehow, she still couldn't quite let the topic go.

"I know, and I appreciate everything you did to open that door for me. It's just that..." She hesitated, but she'd come this far. "I'm not sure it's really the right job for me."

"Of course it is." Her father spoke as if there was no doubt. "You're intelligent, responsible, good with young people. And you're in dire need of a steady income with good health insurance and a solid retirement benefit. This job ticks all the boxes, Cara."

"Except one. I'm just not really that interested in teaching. Nick mentioned something when I took the food over... about how important it is for parents to inspire children to use their gifts. It made me wonder how well I was using mine."

Her father was silent, and for a second or two the only sound was the ponderous ticking of the grandfather clock out in the hallway.

"I see," he said finally. "Is this Nick a parent himself?"

"No," she admitted.

"Then I might question his expertise." Her father sighed. "I know you've been having a very difficult time, Cara. This has been a hard season, the divorce, finishing your degree as a young mother. But you did it, and things are finally beginning to straighten out for you and the boys. Now's not the time to start making impulsive decisions. History's full of people who shipwrecked their lives by following their feelings. Your ex-husband's a prime example."

Cara winced. Her father wasn't wrong. "He wasn't the only one, Dad." The one time in her life when she'd followed her feelings instead of her head was when she'd agreed to drop out of college to get married.

"Maybe not, although personally, I feel his errors were

more serious than yours. Still, all the more reason to learn from past mistakes." He studied her, looking worried. "I'm happy you're enjoying your summer, my dear. This camp is a pleasant diversion for you and the boys. But when summer's over, it'll be time to settle down to more serious work."

The sound of a blowing horn came from outside. The boys were getting impatient.

"I'm sure you're right." She managed a smile. "I'd better hurry. See you this evening."

She silently rehashed the conversation as the boys chattered in the back seat, thinking up all sorts of things she wished she'd said. Which was ridiculous.

Because, of course, her father was exactly right.

Nick wasn't a parent, and he'd never exactly been the responsible sort. Naturally, he'd value happiness over a job that, as her father said, "ticked all the boxes." She couldn't afford to think that way.

She didn't know why it bothered her so much. After all, she'd been perfectly content with the teaching job before. Grateful even.

She was being silly.

The talk with her dad made her a few minutes late, and Nick was waiting at the dining hall when they arrived. He had a trio of stubby fishing poles with him, and—she noticed—two adult-sized poles, as well.

The boys swarmed him. He tousled heads and responded to excited, half-decipherable comments before looking up and meeting her eyes.

His cautious smile hit her like a wave of salty seawater, making her suck in a soft breath. He was leaning against the log wall, framed by a backdrop of green mountains and a morning sky of fragile, robin's egg blue. He'd not fastened his top collar button today, and he looked slightly wrinkled, relaxed and at peace with the world.

Exactly the opposite of how she was feeling at the moment.

"Fishing's probably not your thing, but do you want to join us?" He nodded toward the extra pole. "Might be fun."

He winked, and her heart flipped over. No man should be that good-looking this early in the morning, she decided.

"Yes, Mama!"

"Come with us!"

"Please?"

Her sons chorused their own invitations. Cara opened her mouth to politely refuse—and hesitated.

Nick was right. Fishing most definitely was not her thing. She'd never been fishing in her life—and she'd never wanted to. Worms and muddy water and a flapping fish on the end of a line? No, thank you.

But she recognized this as Nick's version of a peace offering, and suddenly—and for no good reason—she was tempted.

She was so tired of worrying, tired of being sensible and boring and responsible. She wanted to pick up that pole and go with her sons and Nick to the lake and try her hand at fishing. She wanted Nick to laugh at her inability to cast and teach her how to do better. She wanted to enjoy the sun and the water and the summer sunshine for just a few happy minutes, and to still believe—as Nick seemed to—that anything was possible and that following your heart led to happiness.

She wanted that so badly that tears crowded into her eyes, but she swallowed hard and shook her head.

"I have to get breakfast going," she said—even though she'd premixed the dry ingredients for the banana bread pancakes, and it wouldn't take her any time to put them together.

There was a chorus of *aww*s from her boys, but they were too excited to stay disappointed for long. Within seconds, they had their poles in hand and were poised on the path leading to the lake, waiting impatiently for Nick.

She saw a flicker of disappointment in Nick's eyes, too, but he only shrugged and smiled.

"Another time," he said.

She nodded, keeping her smile in place with some difficulty. "Have fun!"

"You, too." There was no sarcasm in Nick's voice. He fully expected her to have fun in the kitchen cooking breakfast.

"Come on, boys," Nick was saying. "We better hurry up before the summer gets away from us!"

He was laughing as he said it, but the words made Cara's stomach turn over. Summer was passing so quickly. And this—all this, the camp, Nick, her cooking job—it was only for the summer.

Then she'd have to go right back to being sensible. And she would. Because her father was right, as usual. Unlike Nick, she had responsibilities—precious ones—that had to come before her own happiness.

But for now, just for today, for this morning, it was still summer. Today she was a camp cook, not a college math instructor.

"You know what?" she heard herself saying. "I think I will go fishing after all. For a little while." She checked her watch. "A half hour or so, maybe. Would that be all right?"

Was she serious?

Nick checked Cara's expression. She looked back at him solemnly.

Of course she was serious. Cara was always serious. He grinned.

"Sure." He handed her the spare pole he'd brought along,

even though he'd doubted she'd go for this idea. "A half hour's great. Come on!"

She considered the pole doubtfully. "Is this all we need? We don't need something to put the fish in?"

"We're not keeping the fish. We're catching and releasing," Nick explained. "Today's all about learning to cast."

"Oh!" She smiled—a real smile this time. She looked at the triplets, who were walking a short distance ahead of them, and lowered her voice. "That's a relief. I wasn't sure what I'd do with live fish if the boys caught any."

He smiled back. "I'm relieved, too. I wasn't sure you'd be speaking to me this morning. I shouldn't have spouted off like I did back at the cabin. I overstepped my bounds a little."

Or a lot.

He'd been worrying about that ever since. Worrying wasn't something he wasted much time on, as a rule. But he'd gone over their conversation several times, replaying what he'd said—and cringing.

He'd never made a habit of sticking his nose in other people's business. If they asked for his help and he could give it, he did. But he respected the right of a person to follow their own course, and he rarely made the mistake of thinking he knew better than they did.

Except, apparently when it came to Cara. Ever since she'd shown up at the camp, he'd been dumping his opinions all over her. That had to stop.

"That's okay," she was saying now.

"No, it's not. I don't have any right to give you advice on the subject of raising kids or anything else."

"Well—" She stopped short as the tip of her pole snagged in the branches drooping overhead. Nick called to the boys to wait and took the rod out of her hands to untangle it.

When he handed it back, that worried pinch had reappeared on her forehead. "I'm sorry. I hope I didn't damage it."

"It's fine." Nick gently pushed the pole down to a lower angle. "Carry it like that. You're less likely to hit branches."

"I'm sorry," she repeated.

"Nothing to be sorry about." Before he could help himself, he added, "And you don't have to apologize every time you make some little mistake. You're entitled to goof up now and then, Cara. Everybody is."

She gave him a quick, sideways glance. "I thought you were done giving me advice."

Good grief, she was right. What was *wrong* with him?

He looked over at her, wondering how to phrase yet another apology. She met his eyes, and the corners of her mouth turned up. She was teasing. His grin broadened.

"You're right," he admitted. "Tell you what. I'll try to stick to fishing advice from here on out. Deal?"

She didn't answer, but her smile bloomed a bit more. They walked along for a few seconds in a companionable silence.

Nick drew in a happy breath. It was a glorious morning, bright and sunny, and barely born. The lake wasn't in view yet, but they were getting close. A faint, fishy freshness blew around them on the morning breeze. And best of all, Cara wasn't irritated with him anymore.

A load had fallen off his shoulders. He was really looking forward to this, he realized. A pleasant half hour or so, fishing on a silent lake with Cara and the boys.

"It wasn't bad advice."

Cara's statement took him by surprise. When he looked at her, she shrugged.

"What you said back at the cabin," she explained. "I actually thought it was...thought-provoking. The idea that it's a parent's job to inspire children, as well as to protect them."

Had he said that? Nick considered. Yeah. He kinda had.

"I'm glad you think so, but like I said. A guy like me has no business offering other people advice on how to live their lives." Especially not somebody like Cara, a single parent of triplets. What did he know about that?

Absolutely nothing, that's what.

"I'm not sure that's true." She slanted a thoughtful glance up at him, her face dappled with leafy shade, her eyes appearing even greener in the gentle morning light. "You seem pretty happy with the choices you've made. Not everybody can say that."

He heard the regret in her voice. She was talking about herself.

"You've made plenty of good choices, Cara." When she made a soft scoffing sound, he doubled down. "You have. There's the proof of it." He nodded toward the boys. "See? They're carrying the poles just like I showed them. A lot of kids nowadays don't want to listen to anybody, much less follow instructions. But yours do."

"You see that as a good thing?" She twinkled another half smile at him. "As I recall, you were never too fond of following instructions yourself."

She wasn't wrong. Back in high school, he'd tested rules for the sake of testing them. He and Cara had butted heads over that more than once. "I've grown up a little since then." He shot her a glance. "A little."

"More than a little, I'd say. You've made a success out of your life."

He laughed. "I wouldn't go that far. Apart from my truck, everything I own fits in two duffel bags." He had some emergency money squirreled away. Not much, but some. Since he was always meeting people who needed money more than he did, it didn't tend to accumulate.

"What you own has nothing to do with how successful you are."

Nick lifted an eyebrow—not because he disagreed. Possessions were nuisances when you moved as often as he did. But he was surprised to hear Cara spouting his own philosophy back to him.

"I mean," she went on, "you've had so many unusual experiences, and you've traveled all over the world. And you've made all kinds of really interesting friends along the way. Missionaries, mercenaries, archeologists, bush pilots, treasure hunters." When he looked at her in surprise, she smiled. "You're a big topic of conversation at the dinner table in my house, remember? The boys repeat the stories you tell."

"Oh." He wasn't entirely sure how he felt about that. "And that—the life I've led—that sounds like success to you?" He was honestly curious—and a little skeptical.

If anybody had asked, Nick would have guessed that Cara's definition of success wouldn't have looked anything like the life he'd chosen.

She shrugged. "It sounds like you were brave enough to live exactly the kind of life you dreamed about. If that isn't success, I don't know what is."

For a second Nick wasn't sure what to say. He'd never cared—never—what other people thought of him. Well, Ruby and his foster siblings—okay, maybe a little. But nobody else. And even those nearest and dearest to his heart had never been allowed to define him. Their opinions had been taken into consideration, sure. But rarely followed. He shrugged praise and criticism off with equal abandon, staying laser focused on whatever he felt called by God to do.

If people were happy with his choices, that was fine. If they weren't—also fine.

But hearing Cara talking about him like that, describing him with that soft approval in her voice?

He liked it.

"I appreciate that." That was an understatement, but it was the closest he dared to go.

They turned a corner in the path, and suddenly the lake stretched out in front of them, sparkling lazily in the summer sun. The boys cheered and broke into a run.

Nick smiled.

"Don't run with those poles!" Cara called. "And don't get too close to the water until a grown-up is nearby! Boys—" She started after them, and before he thought better of it, he reached out and caught her gently by the arm, pulling her to a stop.

"It's okay," he said.

He started to tell her that it was fine, that her boys knew the rules and were good about obeying them, that they were within his sight, and that if anything should go wrong, he could be beside them in seconds.

That he'd never let anything bad happen to her boys. That she could trust him.

He meant to tell her that. But somehow looking down into her face, he forgot all about it.

She stared wide-eyed up at him, startled into stillness, like the deer that he often surprised on his early morning walks. She was so close that he could see a spray of freckles across her nose, faintly golden. He was sure they hadn't been there before. A sweet souvenir of summer, he thought.

He didn't plan to do it. But somehow he found himself tracing the sprinkle with his thumb. And leaning in closer, holding her gaze with his own.

Sploosh.

At the sound of the splash, both of them turned quickly toward the lake.

Chapter Nine

"They're fine," Nick assured Cara. The boys were close to the water, but that edge of the lake was shallow, no more than a foot deep. "They're just skipping stones." He watched as Brian attempted another throw—and the rock splashed into the water without a single skip. He chuckled. "Or trying to."

"Oh." Cara pressed one hand against her heart. She looked dazed—not that he blamed her. He was feeling pretty dazed himself. There for a minute, looking down into her face, he'd forgotten…

Almost everything.

If that splash hadn't come right when it had…

He glanced away from her, back toward the lake, and noticed the boys walking along the waterfront, heading for a deeper section.

"Guys, stay back from the edge there," he called. "Remember the rules. You don't get close to the deep parts without a grown-up nearby."

The triplets all nodded and retraced their steps obediently.

"Rules!" A funny expression crossed Cara's face—an odd mixture of embarrassment and relief. "I don't know what I was thinking. I can't go fishing with you."

"Why not?" Because he'd almost thrown his common sense to the wind and kissed her? Had she figured that out?

Probably. He winced. That made twice he'd nearly gone

off the rails with Cara. He didn't know what had gotten into him, but he needed to get a grip.

And right now he needed to face this head-on and do what damage control he could. He took a breath. "Look, Cara. I shouldn't have—"

"I don't have a fishing license," she interrupted. "You need one to fish in a Georgia park if you're over sixteen. I looked it up when I heard that the boys would be doing some fishing to see if they needed any sort of legal permission. They don't because of their ages, but I would."

This was a first. He'd had to check licenses plenty of times and he'd never seen anybody look so relieved *not* to have one.

Yeah, he'd definitely spooked her.

He sighed and tried for a joke. "Only you."

"What?"

"Only you would be personally invited to fish with a park ranger, and then worry over not having a fishing license."

She looked horrified. "But it's illegal to fish without one."

"It is," he admitted. "And honestly? I just didn't think about it." His brother Logan would have thumped him on the head for forgetting something like that. Logan was as big on rule-following as Cara was.

And they were both right. He was the Red Hawk park ranger, at least for the summer, and this was exactly the sort of thing he was supposed to keep track of. And he had—sort of. He'd double-checked all the counselors and their teen assistants, making sure everybody who'd be on the lake had licenses and were aware of the rules.

But Cara had been a late addition to the staff roster, and anyway, her job description didn't include lake-related activities. Logan had run the requisite background check on her, which had come up squeaky clean, but the idea of a fishing license hadn't occurred to Nick, not even when he'd come up with the idea of inviting her along on this expedition with the boys. He didn't know why he'd forgotten about that.

Well, yeah. Actually he did know why. He kept getting…distracted.

"Never mind," he said. "We can work around it."

Cara shook her head. "I shouldn't set an example of breaking rules."

"Trust me—" That was as far as he got.

"Brian? Aaron? Scott? Come here, please." The boys turned and headed back in her direction. She handed Nick her pole, then knelt so she was at her sons' eye level.

"What's wrong, Mommy?" Aaron asked.

"Nothing," she reassured him. "Except that I forgot something important. Grown-ups need to have a fishing license to fish, and I don't have one. So I won't be able to fish with you guys after all."

"Oh!" Brian frowned, and the little boys exchanged glances.

"But Ranger Nick has one," Scott said hopefully. "Doesn't he?"

Nick didn't miss the uncertain glance Cara sent his way. She wasn't sure if he did or not, he realized. That admiration he'd been so happy to see obviously didn't go very deep. How irresponsible did she think he was?

He probably didn't want to know the answer to that question.

He leaned the poles against a handy tree and dug for his wallet.

"I sure do. See?" He pulled out the fishing license he'd applied for as soon as he'd returned to Georgia for the summer. "That's good for a whole year."

The boys crowded around to view it.

"Are we gonna get one of those?" Scott asked.

"You don't need one," Nick explained. "Kids can fish without a license."

"But Mama can't?"

"No," Cara said. "I can't. So, I'm going to go back to the dining hall and get started on breakfast while you guys have your fishing lesson."

The boys thought this over. "Okay," Brian said. They seemed prepared to accept this change of plans philosophically.

"Do you want me to carry the extra pole back?" Cara offered. "I don't want you to be stuck with it."

"Boys? Can you go wait for me by that rock right there while I talk to your mom for a minute?" He nodded toward a big, flat rock a safe distance from the lake. "See if any lizards are out basking."

"Lizards?" Scott said excitedly. "I like lizards!"

As they jogged happily toward the rock, Nick turned back to Cara.

"Look—" he said.

"I know," she said. "You think I'm being ridiculous, sticking to the rules when nobody would even know if I didn't, but—"

"Would you let me finish a sentence, please?"

His insides were so churned up at the moment that the words came out more curtly than he intended. They served their purpose, though. Cara stopped short.

"Certainly," she said, her tone a few degrees chillier.

"First of all," Nick said, "I don't think you're being ridiculous. I agree with you that it's important to set a good example for kids when it comes to following laws. Especially when nobody would know about it."

"But then why—" Cara started, then subsided when he shot her a look. "Sorry. Go ahead."

"And just so we're clear, I wasn't going to suggest that you fish without a license. I was going to suggest that you fish without bait."

She blinked. "What?"

"With me standing right there, that would have been fine. You could have learned to cast, but you wouldn't technically have been fishing, and you certainly wouldn't have caught anything." He paused, but he'd learned the value of hitting problems head-on, and this one was completely on him. "Anyway we both know this isn't only about a fishing license. I made you uncomfortable just then."

Cara flushed, looking as if she didn't know quite how to answer that. But she didn't deny it, which meant there was only one thing he could say.

"I'm very sorry." He spoke firmly and sincerely. "It won't happen again. Now, I guess I'd better get started on this fishing lesson. We'll see you at breakfast." He picked up the poles and walked toward the boys, leaving her behind.

He didn't want to. He didn't like leaving things like this, but the best he could do at this point was try not to make the situation worse.

And pray that an honest apology and a little space would solve the problem he'd caused.

A week later, Cara wiped down the counters as the campers demolished the breakfast sandwiches she'd prepared. The air in the dining hall was rich with the delicious smells of apples, sausage, coffee and orange juice, and everybody had loved her recipe. She should have been basking in the happy satisfaction of a triumphant cook.

And she would have been. Except for one thing.

Something was wrong with Nick.

She kept sneaking glances in his direction, trying to figure out what was going on.

He sat at a table, surrounded as usual by overexcited children, all jabbering at him while he pushed his food around on his plate. He was smiling, but even from all the way across the room, she could tell that the smile was forced.

That wasn't like Nick. The man smiled as easily as he breathed.

He'd been carefully polite when he'd gone through the serving line, but that wasn't unusual these days. He'd been acting like that for the past week, ever since their botched fishing trip. He hadn't come by for morning coffee since that day, hadn't teased her, not even once.

She never thought she'd miss being teased, but she had to admit, she did. Being teased by Nick had been part of their friendship—and she definitely missed that.

She still wasn't entirely sure what had happened.

She'd replayed that moment by the lake a thousand times in her head, trying to make sense of it, but she hadn't figured it out. They'd been talking, and she'd felt happy—and maybe a little mischievous because she was going fishing instead of working in the kitchen. It felt like skipping a class at school.

Or how she imagined that would have felt if she'd ever actually done it.

She'd felt peaceful, too. She'd found more peace at camp than she'd expected. She wasn't really the outdoorsy type, but there was something about having a close-up, daily view of God's gorgeous creation that settled her heart and calmed her anxiety.

Well, that was part of it.

But, if she was being completely honest, part of it was also because of the man she'd been walking next to. There was something relaxing about Nick's company. He always seemed so completely at ease with himself and the world, so ready to enjoy whatever came.

Of course, she'd been keeping an eye on the boys because they were, after all, her responsibility, and so naturally she'd started after them when they'd broken into a run. And Nick had caught her arm and told her it was okay.

She remembered that part very clearly. That was all he'd said. *It's okay.* But somehow, as he'd looked into her face, she'd felt as if he wasn't only talking about the boys.

For a second there, she'd felt—and this was the silly part—as if he was talking about everything, her whole confusing, mixed-up, disappointing life. That it was all okay. Not only what had happened in the past, but what was happening now: feeling happy, enjoying a new friendship, going on an unplanned fishing excursion instead of triple-checking her breakfast preparations.

Then out of the blue he'd touched her face, gently. She was sure he hadn't meant anything by it, but suddenly the whole bright, green, summery world around her had shrunk down to just… Nick.

That feeling was so unexpected and so strong that it had startled her. Scared her a little, too. She shouldn't feel that way about Nick. They were friends. It was silly.

But that wasn't the strangest part.

The strangest thing was that, just for a second or two, she'd seen something in his eyes that made her wonder if maybe she wasn't the only one feeling a little…silly.

And that idea…which maybe she'd imagined…well. It had sent her nerves into such a frenzy that she'd barely been able to think.

Then they'd heard that startling splash, and everything had fallen apart fast. She'd been frightened for the boys—until she'd seen they were all right. And that moment with Nick, innocent as it was, had left her feeling unsteady, as if she'd been on one of those whirly rides at the fair. She'd been thankful to think of the excuse of the fishing license to cut the outing short.

Somebody else might have understood and accepted it politely. Not Nick. Not only had he seen right through her excuse, he'd called her on it.

That meant he'd seen how unraveled she'd been, which was mortifying.

He'd apologized for making her uncomfortable and promised it wouldn't happen again. And it hadn't. He'd kept a very careful distance between them ever since, although as near as she could tell, he'd been his usual friendly self with the children, including her three boys. They'd trotted home with their usual repertoire of Nick stories each afternoon.

But today he seemed different, even with the kids. Subdued. That wasn't like Nick at all, and it was worrying her.

The table across from him emptied as the campers finished eating and moved to dump their trays and head outside. Cara hesitated for a second, then rinsed out her rag with hot water and went to wipe it down.

She didn't mean to eavesdrop—exactly. But, of course, being that close, she couldn't help overhearing conversations.

"Ain't you hungry, Ranger Nick?" A skinny boy next to him eyed Nick's uneaten food with concern. His own plate was scraped so clean it looked as if it had been washed. "The food's real good."

Nick looked up from his plate. He smiled, but the smile didn't reach his eyes. "I'm not too hungry today, Riley."

"I could finish that for you," he offered. "I mean, if you ain't gonna eat it."

"Are you still hungry, bud? Go on up and get another sandwich, a whole one. I'm sure Miss Cara has plenty left." Nick glanced up at her, a question in his eyes.

"I sure do," Cara said cheerfully. She made a point of

making extra food. These kids often came to camp very hungry. "Help yourself, Riley. You'd be doing me a favor. You know how I hate to see good food go to waste." She heard a whistle and glanced out the big screens at the groups organizing themselves outside. "Looks like your counselor is about ready to lead your group off, so maybe wrap the sandwich up in a paper towel. That way you can take it with you."

Riley's face brightened. "Thanks!" He headed up to the serving station, leaving Nick alone at the table.

Cara hesitated for a second, then decided enough was enough.

"Okay." She dropped down on the bench across from him. "What's going on? Are you sick?"

He shook his head, offering that same wooden smile he'd been giving her for a week. "I feel fine. Just got a lot on my mind."

She started to ask him if it was something he'd want to talk about, but then she reconsidered. Whatever Nick's problem was, she apparently wasn't the person he wanted to discuss it with.

So she nodded and rose to go back into the kitchen. The dining hall cleared out rapidly as the remaining campers finished breakfast and hurried outside, eager to get onto the day's activities. They rushed past, faces and shirts bearing the evidence of well-enjoyed breakfasts, their eyes shining.

"See you later, Mama!" Scott said as her boys rushed past.

"See you, sweeties," she called after them. "Have fun!"

Several other campers greeted her, too, and many offered fist bumps to Nick as they hurried past. As the last of the kids exited, the noise level dropped dramatically. Nick sighed and got up from the table.

"Time to get to work," he said. "Thanks for breakfast."

She nodded, although she'd seen him dump most of it into the trash. Usually Nick didn't like to waste food any more than she did.

Whatever was on his mind, it was bugging him. A lot.

"You know," she said suddenly, making her tone brisk. "That lizard is back."

Nick paused, halfway to the door. "What?"

"The lizard." She kept her eyes down, rummaging for a plastic container to put the breakfast leftovers in. "He's in the pantry again. Our deal was that I provide fresh coffee and the occasional biscuit, and you're in charge of varmint removal." She lifted an eyebrow at him as she snapped the lid on the container of breakfast sandwiches. "Coffee's been made every single morning, but you haven't been keeping up your end of the bargain. I had to kill three spiders and shoo out a bird all by myself this week." She made a face. "And the spiders were really big."

For the first time in a week, she saw a faint, familiar twinkle in his eye. "Looks like you survived."

"That's not the point. Killing spiders isn't in my job description." She kept her tone light. "I'm the cook. You're the creepy-crawly wrangler. You don't want to deal with the lizard, fine. But if he jumps out at me one more time, I might just pack up my spoon and my spatula, and you'll be stuck doing the cooking all by yourself. We both know how *that* would turn out."

Nick studied her. As their eyes met, one corner of his mouth tipped up, flashing that hint of a dimple.

"We also both know you'd never let me take over this kitchen, not in a million years. So why don't you stop making empty threats and show me where you saw the lizard last?"

Chapter Ten

Nick scooted cans around in the pantry. "This is where he was?"

"Yes, right on that shelf."

"Well, there's no sign of him now. I hate to break it to you, but lizards are tough to catch. The good news is, he's probably not doing much damage. In fact, he's likely eating a lot of bugs, which is a good thing."

"The spiders were out there." She nodded toward the kitchen. "I haven't seen any bugs in here."

"Of course not." He winked. "Because you have a lizard."

Cara made a face at him. Then she bit her lip and appeared to be weighing her options. "Okay," she said after a second. "If he's eating bugs, I guess you can leave him alone. I just hate it when I come in here after something and he…you know." She shuddered. "Scurries away."

In spite of the heaviness in his chest today, Nick smiled. "Would you rather he scurried closer?"

"Definitely not." Another shudder. "Don't lizards carry diseases?"

"Are you planning to pick him up?"

"No!"

"Then I think you're fine." Nick moved the cans back into place—because he knew if he didn't, Cara would the minute he left. The pantry looked as if it'd been alphabetized. He turned and found himself face-to-face with her, only a few feet between them.

Which was plenty of space, really—or it should have been. It was a roomy pantry, but for some reason, with them both in there, it felt small. He could smell Cara's perfume—a delicate, floral scent that reminded him of mimosa blossoms.

He'd always loved that scent. Here in Georgia when the mimosas bloomed, it had meant school was out for the summertime—his favorite time of year because it meant freedom. Even now, the smell gave him a sense of happy anticipation.

He cleared his throat. "If that's all you wanted, I'd better—"

"There's one more thing." She tilted her head. "I'd like to ask you a personal question."

A personal question. His mind flashed back to that moment beside the lake. He hoped the question didn't have anything to do with that.

Because he didn't have any answers for her—at least not any that made sense.

"Shoot," he said, with more bravado than he felt.

"What's wrong with you today, Nick? And don't say nothing because something definitely is. You're not yourself."

He lifted an eyebrow. She was worried about him? He wasn't expecting that. He was surprised—he thought he'd done a pretty good job of covering up how worried he was.

"I've got a lot on my mind."

"So you said. Do you want to talk about it? I don't mean to be nosy, but..." She sounded suddenly shy. "You were so nice to me when I was upset. I'd be happy to return the favor. Sometimes it helps to have a listening ear."

He started to say no, thanks. He'd been working hard for the past week to keep a nice, professional distance with Cara. Talking about his personal problems wasn't professional. *No* was the right answer.

But when he opened his mouth, what came out instead was, "I'm getting worried about Ruby."

Cara's expression immediately shifted into concern. "What's going on?" She leaned back against the shelf behind her, arms crossed in front of her apron, as if she'd settled in to stay, ready to hear the whole story.

To his surprise, he found himself telling it. How Ruby was looking gray-faced and pinched these days and got out of breath far too easily. How she wasn't eating well, and the worst thing of all—how last night she'd told him that she'd started planning his memory quilt.

"Your memory quilt?" Cara looked confused.

"She's making one for all of us." He shot her a wary glance. "Out of bits and pieces of our old clothes. She gives them as wedding presents, so usually, when she starts working on one, it's tied to one of her matchmaking schemes."

Cara blinked. "Ruby's trying to find you a wife?"

"No, that's just it. She isn't. We talked about it a while back. But she's started working on a quilt for me anyway."

"And that's a bad thing?"

"The quilt's not bad, but her reason for making it early worries me. When I asked her, she said she wasn't about to 'go to glory' as she puts it and leave me the only one of her kids without his own quilt."

It was hard to tell that part without choking up. He remembered the determined look on his foster mom's tired face when she'd made that pronouncement.

He also remembered how his heart had sunk like a stone. He knew what this meant. Ruby could tell him all day long that she was fine, that she was feeling better, that he didn't have to worry. This quilt thing, though. This told him the truth.

Ruby suspected she was dying.

He'd tried to joke with her about it, to see if she'd set

aside the idea. *Thought I was supposed to find myself a bride first, Ruby.*

She'd waved aside that objection. *Can't wait on that, Nicky. 'Course I'd sure like to see the young lady you end up with. She's bound to be something special. But time's getting by, and you ain't showing no signs of settling down. A quilt will keep. Now, you don't have to worry about hauling it around the world. I'll store it right here at home for you, and when the time comes, it'll be ready and waiting.*

Whether I'm here or not. She hadn't said that part. But he'd heard it.

"Has she been to see the doctor?" Cara asked, a familiar pucker of concern between her brows.

Normally he didn't like to see it, but right now there was something comforting about that little wrinkle. It showed she cared.

He shook his head. "Not too recently. She has a checkup scheduled in a couple of weeks. We've tried to get her to push it up, but so far she's been stubborn. She says she's too busy with Torey's wedding stuff to fuss over doctor's appointments."

"That's right. Torey's wedding is coming up pretty soon. Well, no wonder Ruby's feeling a little run-down. There's so much to do, for one thing. And a wedding's such an emotional time for a mom. At least," Cara added, "I'd imagine it would be."

She spoke matter-of-factly, but he remembered that her own mother had passed away long before her own wedding. There would have been no mom to help her prep and plan for her big day.

He wondered if she'd missed that. Probably so. He felt a pang of sympathy.

"Maybe you're right." The idea made him feel a little

better. If Ruby's uncharacteristic weariness was wedding related, maybe the problem would resolve itself.

"Once the wedding is safely over with, Ruby will probably perk up. And if not, it'll be about time for her appointment, and her doctor will check her out thoroughly, I'm sure."

The more he thought that over, the better he felt. "I think you're onto something. Ruby has been fussing over a lot of details. Torey couldn't care less about most of them, but that just seems to make Ruby care more. Of course, she's had plenty of help. Charlotte and Maggie are both pitching in. But Ruby always insists on being in the middle of things."

Cara smiled. "Well, weddings have lots of moving parts, so I'm sure there are plenty of responsibilities to go around. There are the flowers and the dresses and the food and the guest lists. Of course, I'm sure Maggie's handling the food, and I've heard that Charlotte designed Torey's gown herself. I'm sure it'll be beautiful."

He glanced at her sharply. She sounded almost…wistful. An idea occurred to him.

It was a bad idea. A risky idea. An idea that, likely, would undo all that damage control he'd been working on for the past week.

So, of course, he went with it.

"Want to go?"

She blinked at him. "What?"

"To the wedding? Want to go? I have a plus-one, and nobody to take. The girls have been fussing at me about that." Why it mattered so much to his sisters that he bring a date, he couldn't imagine, but over the past few weeks he'd learned that all sorts of silly things mattered to women when it came to weddings.

Cara stared at him, her mouth drooping open. She'd already taken her apron off, revealing khaki shorts and a Red Hawk

Camp T-shirt. Her hair was tied back in a blue bandanna. She looked pretty, he thought. Natural and bright-eyed—and startled.

"You want me to go to Torey's wedding with you?" she asked now.

Well, yeah. He thought he'd been plenty clear. Then he realized what she was really asking.

"As a friend," he said quickly. "Not a date. And I'd owe you one. You'd be doing me a favor, getting my sisters off my back."

"Oh!" She nodded. "Well, of course. In that case, I'd be happy to." She said something else about letting her know about the time and all that, but he barely heard her. He was laser focused on something else.

There in Cara's eyes, just for a second, he could've sworn he saw disappointment. Not much, just a flicker, right when he'd said the part about going as friends.

Later he wasn't sure what else he said to her or how he got out of the pantry and the dining hall, but somehow he managed it. He was halfway down the trail to the ranger's office before he clocked back in.

He took a quick inventory and was pleasantly surprised. The weight that had been pressing down on his chest since his supper with Ruby yesterday had lifted. The sun was bright and warm, and the air was fresh and sharp with the tang of the pines rustling in the breeze overhead.

The world seemed a better place than it had just a few hours ago, and he knew why. Cara had closed the gap he'd put between them. That was part of it. And the other part—if he was honest with himself—was that little flash of disappointment when he'd said they'd be going to the wedding as friends.

He was still thinking about that when he walked into

his office, slid into his desk chair and tapped his computer to life.

Time to get busy. He had plenty to do, and he was always behind on paperwork.

But instead, he pulled up his emails on his phone and reread the one that had come last night from the coordinator of Hope for Healing, asking Nick to call him about a job heading up the building of a clinic in El Salvador.

It was the third time the guy had reached out. Nick had worked on similar projects with this foundation, and he knew this clinic was being built in a particularly unstable and mountainous area. The construction was likely to encounter hostility from humans and nature alike. Nick was a great pick for this kind of assignment, and he knew it. Danger didn't put him off, and he had plenty of experience managing both angry people and treacherous terrain.

Since the clinic was desperately needed—and since he respected the man in charge of the project—this should have been an automatic yes. He'd already mentioned it to his family, who'd accepted the news philosophically.

But for some reason, he hadn't said yes officially yet. He probably should. Instead, he sat there for a long time, rereading the email and thinking about that look in Cara's eyes.

When he finally picked up the phone, he didn't dial the coordinator's number. He dialed his brother Logan's.

When Logan answered, Nick went straight to the point. "This park ranger job. Have you filled it yet? Permanently, I mean."

"Not yet. Why?"

"No promises, but—" Nick sucked in a deep breath "—forward me the application."

Three days later, Cara slid her carefully constructed breakfast pizzas into the large oven and began cleaning up.

Coffee was dripping into the carafe of the coffee maker, adding an energizing scent to the muggy air.

It was mid-July now, and the days got hot early. She was turning on the large fans that cooled the dining hall even before the campers showed up for breakfast. Camp was almost over. Only a couple more weeks to go.

She wiped the counters a little harder, a hollow ache in her middle at the thought. She was going to miss this so much.

On impulse, she put down the rag and walked to the large, screened windows that looked over the camp. The sun was already well up, its light muffled by an overcast sky. They'd had rain overnight. Its fresh smell still hung in the air, and droplets dripped off the leaves, leaving dark splotches on the mulch paths.

She'd never been much of an outdoorsy person, and she still wasn't a huge fan of slithery, crawly creatures that wouldn't stay outside where they belonged. The lizard had put in another appearance this morning and scared her half to death. She was trying to appreciate him for his bug-eating service, but it wasn't easy.

Still, lizards aside, Red Hawk Camp was a beautiful place. She'd loved her time here. There was something special about doing simple, honest work that she enjoyed in a place dedicated to helping children from struggling families.

Like her own.

She'd come here praying that this camp would heal her boys, but God had given her more than she'd asked for. The place had healed her, too. She was sad at the thought of it ending, but already there were signs everywhere that camp was coming to a close. The pantry was emptying out, flyers were going home reminding the parents of the end of the camp bonfire and assembly, the counselors were talking more and more about what they'd be doing in the fall.

Except for Nick. He hadn't said much.

She'd waited for it, expecting that he'd start describing his next big adventure, but he'd remained curiously silent. Of course, Torey's wedding was the day after the last day of camp, and Ruby's doctor's appointment was the week after that. He was probably waiting to see how all that turned out.

"Cara?"

She glanced to the left and lifted her eyebrows. Nick was picking his way out of the woods. Not his usual path in the morning, but, of course, that was Nick. He wasn't exactly predictable.

"Ready for coffee?" she asked with a smile.

"In a minute. What kind of shoes do you have on?"

She looked down at her feet. "Tennis shoes. Why?"

"Those'll do. Come on. There's something I want to show you."

Cara glanced back at the kitchen. At least another thirty minutes on the pizzas, and most everything else was done. But she hadn't put on any bug spray, and that path Nick had come up didn't look much like a path at all. Lots of underbrush and low-hanging branches.

And there might be—likely would be—snakes.

She shuddered and looked at Nick, about to tell him that probably this wasn't the best idea. But he smiled at her, his brown eyes sparkling with something—excitement or mischief, she couldn't really tell.

And, she realized, she didn't really care. Whatever he wanted to show her, she wanted to see.

"Okay, but I'll need to be back in half an hour," she told him as she walked up the slope to where he was standing. "Or our breakfast pizzas will be briquettes."

"No problem." Nick pulled back a branch so she could pass. "It's not far."

They crunched through pine needles, Nick leading the

way. He kept a sharp eye, pointing out stones or stumps that she should step around.

She needed him to point them out because she didn't have eyes for anything much but Nick himself.

He'd always been inconveniently good-looking. Back in high school, she'd credited his looks and his charm for getting him out of most of the messes he'd gotten himself into, and she privately thought he was much more handsome now. He had a nicely cut face, a strong, straight blade of a nose, high cheekbones, and the chin of a man who was comfortable making his own decisions.

But it was more than just that.

There was a strength in his jaw, a reassuring broadness to his shoulders and a calm certainty in the way he moved. He seemed completely at home in the woods, and she felt safe with him—even though it really did look rather snakey through here.

But if a snake showed up, she felt sure Nick would see it and deal with it. And then tease her about being afraid of it.

His eyes danced when they were teasing—and they often were. But there was a kindness in him, too, a gentle chivalry that she'd never noticed back in high school. At first, she'd told herself Nick had changed over the years. Now she wasn't so sure.

Maybe that kindness had always been there, underneath. Maybe she'd simply never looked closely enough to see it.

Nick halted and held one arm out, signaling her to stop, too.

"What—" she started, but he held his finger to his lips, nodding toward a tangled cluster of briars ahead of them.

It took her a minute to see it. When she did, she sucked in her breath in a soft, awed gasp.

There, nestled in the fallen leaves, was a young fawn, still dappled with white spots. Ferns fringed her little bed, and pale sunlight fingered its way through the clouds to spotlight the small creature. As they watched, it raised its delicate head and studied them innocently, its ears quirked upward, looking too big for its narrow face.

"Oh, my," she whispered. Without thinking, she reached out and squeezed Nick's arm. "She's so beautiful. I've never seen one this close. But why's she here all alone? Where's her mama?"

Nick smiled down at her. "Off grazing. White-tailed does stash their babies in a safe place and then go off to eat."

"Isn't that dangerous? Something could find her and hurt her."

"Maybe," he murmured. "But mama deer have good instincts. She'll have checked this place out carefully, smelled it over. That's why we won't go too close, so she'll keep using this spot."

They stood there for a few more minutes, watching the little fawn. She considered them with big brown eyes, then, apparently convinced they weren't anything to worry herself about, she twitched her ears and settled her nose back down on her forelegs to continue her nap.

Finally Nick tapped his watch. Time for them to go. Reluctantly, Cara turned around and they began walking back toward the camp.

"How did you find her?" she asked when they were a safe distance away.

"I was wandering the woods, checking things. Happened across her, and I thought maybe you'd like to see."

"Thank you," Cara said, her mind still on the beautiful little scene. "Is something wrong? That you're checking on things in the woods?" She didn't recall Nick doing anything like that before.

He took a few steps before he answered. "Not wrong, no. I'm just...looking the park over."

That was a curiously evasive answer. "Why?"

"Mind your step." He nodded toward a stump in front of them. As she stepped around it, she realized something.

She was still holding Nick's arm.

She flushed. But when she loosened her fingers, to her astonishment, he pressed his other hand over hers and held it there.

He stopped walking and looked down at her.

"Cara," he said. "I…uh…" He glanced off over the woods. "The reason that I'm walking over the park is because I'm applying for the ranger job here."

Her heart jumped, hard, with hope—and surprise. "You're staying in Cedar Ridge?"

"Nothing's settled. I'm just putting in an application. There are a lot of details to work out."

Her mind raced. Nick in Cedar Ridge long term. That was…

She didn't know exactly what that was. Exciting. Dangerous.

Wonderful.

"Oh," she managed. A thought occurred to her. "Is it because you're worried about Ruby?"

"That's part of it," Nick said. "This trip home has reminded me that Ruby's not going to be here forever. I don't like the idea of missing any time with her."

Cara nodded. She could understand that.

Nick hesitated. "But it's not the only reason. So, before I go too far with this idea, I'd like to know…"

"What?" Her heart was beating so hard she wondered if he could hear it.

"If you've got some room for me in your life," he said simply. "Just that. I'm not asking for…anything else. But I'd like to spend time with you and the boys while I'm here. If that would be okay with you."

She started to say yes. Of course it would be okay with her. Better than okay.

But then that little phrase he'd just used—*while I'm here*—registered.

Nick was telling her he was staying longer. Not that he was staying forever.

Nick the Nomad never stayed anywhere forever. And the longer he stayed, the harder it would be—for her and her sons—to see him go.

He was waiting for her answer. She stared up at him, unsure what she ought to say.

"Nick!" The urgent call came from the direction of the camp. They both turned in that direction.

Another voice picked it up. "Nick?"

"Here!" Nick called back. "Hang on. Coming your way!"

They moved swiftly down the slope, toward the camp. When they broke through the edge of the woods, two of the adult counselors were waiting, their faces set in serious lines.

Cara's skin prickled. Something was wrong.

Nick's face had gone white. "What is it?"

"Your brother's been trying to get you on your phone," one of the counselors said. "He finally called us and asked us to find you."

"I silenced it." Nick said. So as not to startle the fawn, Cara realized. A muscle jumped in his jaw. "Ruby?"

The man nodded. "I'm sorry, yeah. They've rushed her to the hospital here in town, but they're moving her to Atlanta. And, Nick? Logan says you'd better come quick."

Chapter Eleven

Nick had never hated hospitals. If anything, he considered himself a fan. He'd helped build them in various parts of the world—and been a patient in more than a few, thanks to accidents and tropical illnesses. He'd figured out ingenious ways to transport injured people and much-needed supplies to them. And he'd been in too many parts of the world where modern medical care wasn't accessible not to deeply appreciate them and the skilled doctors and nurses who staffed them.

But right now in this waiting room, anxious to hear how Ruby's emergency heart surgery was going, he was as miserable as he'd ever been in his life.

She'd collapsed at home that morning, and it had been some time before she'd been found. Nick blamed himself for that. About half the time he stopped by Ruby's house before leaving for camp, but he'd had a lot of thinking to do today. Ruby would have picked up on his mood and asked questions, and he didn't have any answers to give her yet.

So he'd skipped the stop.

Thankfully Logan's wife, Charlotte, had called about some sort of wedding nonsense, and when she hadn't been able to get Ruby on the phone, she'd dispatched Logan to check on her. He'd found Ruby unconscious on the kitchen linoleum, a shattered coffee cup beside her.

Her *World's Best Mom* mug, Logan had said. Nick didn't

like remembering the expression on his brother's face when he'd said that—a look he'd known was mirrored on his own.

"We'll get her a new one," he'd promised Logan fiercely.

Due to the seriousness of the situation, Ruby had been life-flighted from the smaller local hospital to Southeastern General here in Atlanta. A top-notch cardiologist had evaluated her and decided that emergency surgery was called for. Forms had been signed, and all the legalities dealt with.

Now it was late afternoon, and the family was not so patiently waiting for word in the designated room.

Or in Nick's case, pacing from one end of the space to the other while his foster siblings clustered with their spouses, holding hands so tightly that their knuckles were white.

"Sit down, Nick." His sister Maggie patted the empty chair on her left. Her husband, Neil, was seated on her right, his face set in grim, sympathetic lines, balancing a box from Angelo's on his knees. Nobody ever went hungry on Maggie's watch. "You'll wear out the carpet."

"Let him be." His brother Ryder ran a hand roughly through his hair. "I'm about to climb the walls myself." His wife, Elise, patted his arm.

"No news is good news," she said gently.

"I'm trying to believe that," his sister Jina said tearfully. "But it's been so long. Weren't they supposed to give us updates?" Her new husband put his arm around her shoulders and drew her against his chest, resting his chin on her hair.

"I'll go check." Patrick, Torey's fiancé, rose to his feet. She jumped up, too.

"I'm going with you," she said, but he shook his head.

"I saw you eyeing that computer at the nurses' station. If you get half a chance, you'll hack into the hospital system to find out Ruby's condition." Patrick's tone was teasing, but there was an undertone of seriousness. Torey was a computer genius, and she was as desperate for news as the rest of them. "If I let you anywhere near a keyboard, you'll get us arrested or at the very least thrown out of here."

"Only if I get caught," Torey muttered, but she sank back into her chair. Patrick leaned down to press a kiss on her forehead.

"I'll come with you," Ryder said.

"Let him go," Elise suggested, and there was a murmur of agreement. His brother's easygoing personality made him a stellar salesman, and if his charm could score them some early information about Ruby's status, they'd take it.

As his two brothers started down the hall, Nick watched the rest of his family closing ranks. Elise moved next to Torey, closing the gap their husbands had left. Jina and Maggie leaned against their own husbands, and Charlotte stroked Logan's arm gently, her eyes fixed on his set, worried face.

Everybody had somebody special with them. Somebody to bear this awful waiting, and the hovering, horrible fear that Ruby might not be coming home.

Everybody but him.

"I'll be back in a minute," he said.

"Keep your phone on," Logan replied. "I'll let you know when there's news."

Nick nodded. As he walked away, Jina murmured something he couldn't make out.

"He just needs some time alone," Maggie said gently. "You know how Nick is."

He clenched his jaw as he strode down the hospital corridors. Because she was wrong.

He didn't need time to himself. He needed somebody to sit next to him and hold his hand and help him face a future that might not include Ruby.

He needed what they all had.

He walked, not caring much where he went, until he noticed a sign reading Chapel. He turned and pushed through the door into a small, hushed room with two arched stained glass windows at the front and short rows of padded pews.

Nobody else was there.

Nick had visited many different places of worship during his travels. He made a point of that, actually. He'd learned that part of making his not-so-ordinary life work was taking the most important parts of himself with him wherever he happened to go. His faith was an essential he never left behind.

Maybe he never stuck around long enough to become a regular at any particular church, but he loved connecting with other believers wherever he happened to be. He also enjoyed experiencing the different forms that church took in various parts of the world.

He'd worshipped God in huts and caves, on the edge of the ocean and on the top of a mountain. He'd worshiped in secret because it was illegal, and he'd participated in public celebrations of faith that brought whole towns together.

He'd reached for God in a hundred very different places, but one thing had always been the same, a sense of soul-deep peace that pushed past whatever trouble he happened to be fighting at that particular moment.

He felt that here, too, in this cramped room that was plain and empty and smelled like industrial-strength antiseptic. He sat down in a pew and faced the altar, unadorned except for a simple cross engraved on the front. He cleared his throat.

"God," he said quietly. "You know why I'm here. We're worried about Ruby, all of us. You already gave her to us once, years ago, because we needed her." A tiny smile tickled at the memories. "Most of us didn't know how much we needed her back then. But You knew. So I think You must know now that we still need her. Especially me. I'm just…not ready yet to let her go." He paused, remembering the scene in the waiting room, all his siblings huddled with their loved ones.

In his mind he heard Ruby's words echoing. *I ain't gonna be around forever, Nicky. It's time you found yourself a sweetheart and settled down.*

This, he realized, was exactly what Ruby had been preparing for. The tireless woman who'd taken a raggedy bunch of sullen teens and turned them into a family had done her best to usher them into new families, families of their own, before she left them.

They'd all laughed about her matchmaking, teased her, resisted her. He hadn't understood until this second what an act of love it had been. Only Ruby, who had such a knack for seeing into hurt and guarded hearts, could have fully understood how important it was for her hard-to-place fosterlings to have other people to love and belong to when she was gone.

If God called Ruby home today—and the doctor had been clear that this was a possibility—he wouldn't be alone. He'd have his faith, of course, and he'd also have his family. The five foster siblings he'd grown to love would be there for him, and their marriages had expanded his family circle even more. There would be good people around him, people who cared and who'd be grieving alongside him. People whose homes would be open to him whenever he blew back into town, for as long as he wanted to stay.

That was true.

But he also understood that, in a way, yeah, he'd be very much alone when the little white farmhouse on the top of Sawyer's mountain was empty. Alone in a way none of his siblings were, not anymore.

"Nick?"

A voice spoke softly behind him. He turned to see Cara standing at the door, twisting her hands together.

"I'm sorry," she said. "I went up to the waiting room, and nobody seemed to know exactly where you were." She hesitated. "I don't want to disturb you."

He got to his feet. "You're not disturbing me at all."

She took a few steps forward. "Logan said, if I found you, to tell you that the nurses are expecting the surgeon to come out with an update in just a few minutes."

His heart thudded. "All right."

It was time to face...whatever he had to face. But now, Cara was here.

And somehow, that helped.

He walked toward her. The colored squares from the stained glass window had fallen on the carpet, making a little path leading in her direction. In spite of the tension building in his gut, he almost laughed out loud.

Then he remembered what Ruby had said about Cara not being the right woman for him. Or more accurately, his not being the right man for her.

And his smile faded.

He looked into Cara's face. "It's a long drive from Cedar Ridge to Atlanta." And not an easy one. Atlanta traffic was notorious.

He left the statement hanging.

Cara looked uncomfortable. "I know. And maybe I should have...checked first before coming. But I knew you were worried about Ruby, and I thought maybe having a friend here might help. I knew you'd have your family with you, but—" She shot him an uncertain look. "After the triplets were born, they had to stay in the NICU a long time. I didn't have too many friends but there was an older lady at my church who came and sat with me every day." A tiny smile. "She brought her knitting. We didn't...say much. But it was really comforting to have somebody there in my corner."

He started to ask where her husband had been, then thought better of it. Best to leave the past in the past.

"I'm glad you're here, Cara." And he was. Oddly, deeply, humbly glad. "But how did you know where to find me?" He hadn't told anybody he was going to the chapel. In fact, he hadn't known he was going himself.

She looked embarrassed. "I guessed. If you'd left your family, I figured it was because you wanted to go off by yourself and pray for your mom. If there'd been a garden I'd have looked there first, but there wasn't. So when I saw the chapel on the hospital map, I came here."

The fact that she'd known just where to look for him… It touched him. Who else would have known that? That he'd likely seek peace first in green places, and then in a church.

Nobody, probably. Except maybe Ruby.

"We'd better go up to the waiting room," Cara suggested gently. "You'll want to be with your family to hear what the doctor has to say."

He wasn't so sure he wanted to hear what the doctor would say. They'd tried to be optimistic, but the somber look on the surgeon's face when he'd spoken to them earlier hadn't been reassuring.

He squared his shoulders. "You're right," he said. "Let's go."

As they left the chapel, he took her hand. She looked up at him in surprise, but she didn't pull her hand free. Instead, her fingers twined trustingly, comfortingly in his.

He looked down the corridor that led back to the waiting room—and news that he wasn't sure he was prepared for. But he was sure of one thing.

Whatever lay ahead, good news or bad, he was thankful to have Cara beside him as he faced it.

They got to the waiting room a few seconds too late. The surgeon was already striding away, and his foster siblings were huddled in a circle. Torey was the one facing him, Patrick's arm around her shoulders, and when he saw the tears on his sister's face, his heart fell to his shoes.

Unlike Maggie and Jina, Torey almost never cried.

But then her eyes caught his, and a shaky smile lit her face, and he knew what the surgeon had said before anybody spoke a word.

Ruby was going to pull through.

The following Monday at lunchtime, Cara stood in the dining hall kitchen and watched the children devouring her variation on the pineapple chicken kebabs. She'd deconstructed them and was serving them over a mound of fluffy rice.

She hadn't been sure how well they'd be received because she'd noticed that the children celebrated the simpler foods…hamburgers, hot dogs, chicken fingers.

She'd detected some dubious looks, but they'd trusted her enough to taste it. She'd sweetened the deal by making a layered chocolate cookie and pudding dessert—complete with gummy worms—that she knew would be a huge hit.

Going by the scraped-clean plates, the whole lunch had passed muster. She smiled, wishing Nick had been here to taste it and see the solution she'd come up with.

He hadn't kept regular hours at the camp over the past several days, and, of course, she understood why. Ruby, according to his texts and a couple of brief phone calls, was recovering well from the surgery to replace a faulty heart valve. Due to her age and her run-down condition, though, her convalescence would take time, and her foster kids and their spouses were leaving nothing to chance. They were taking turns staying with her at the hospital and were busy interviewing various companies that offered home health services so that she could have the best possible nursing care once she returned home.

She understood all that. And she thought it was sweet how determined Nick and the rest of them were to take care of the woman who'd stepped in to take care of them.

On the other hand, Nick's absence had left certain things…hanging.

As the campers finished their lunches and headed out the door, she returned their greetings and smiled at their compliments, but her mind drifted back to that moment in the hospital chapel when Nick had reached out to take her hand.

That had been so unexpected. She hadn't been sure that she should go to the hospital at all. But she'd remembered Nick's face when he'd heard about Ruby. After countless hospital vigils with her sons, she'd understood that stricken expression, and she knew the pain behind it. So she'd left the boys with her dad and driven to Atlanta.

To her relief, Nick had been glad to see her. She'd read that much in his face—and she hadn't missed the startled looks his siblings had exchanged when she'd arrived. It was clear they were curious, but, of course, they'd been too concerned about Ruby to spend much time thinking about anything else. In fact, she doubted they'd given her unexpected arrival much thought since, which was probably a good thing, at least until she and Nick figured this out themselves.

She wasn't doing a very good job of that. No matter how much she turned all this over in her head—the things Nick had said after he'd taken her to see the fawn, the way he'd held her hand all the way up that long hospital corridor—she couldn't quite make sense out of it.

She wanted to make sense out of it. But for that to happen, she and Nick would have to talk, face-to-face, and time was running out.

Outside, the summer still seemed to be in full swing, but there was no debating the calendar. This was the last week of camp. She was trying not to dwell on that fact, but it loomed in the back of her mind. There was going to be a special presentation and bonfire on Friday night for the campers and their parents, and that would be the end of it all. It would be time to hang up her spatula and her big cooking spoon and break out her math textbooks.

And start collecting a nice, steady paycheck, she reminded herself.

God, please help me to enjoy teaching, she prayed silently as she cleaned up the kitchen. *Help me to be a blessing to my students.*

She had just finished putting the kitchen to rights when she heard a faint, familiar noise. She cocked her head listening hard. Then a smile broke over her face.

She recognized that whistled tune. Nick was coming up the path.

Sure enough, he was at the door in half a minute, not in his uniform today. He was wearing jeans and a simple blue cotton shirt. He looked tired, and his dark hair needed a trim, but his eyes lit up at the sight of her.

She smiled at him, wanting to say—to ask—a thousand things all at once. Instead she blurted out the first thing that occurred to her.

"You missed lunch."

"Sorry. I wanted to get here earlier, but Ruby was moved to the rehab wing of the hospital today," he told her. "I stayed to get her settled."

"How's she doing?"

"Great." His smile flashed, teasing the almost-dimple out of hiding. "This move was way ahead of schedule, but it's what Ruby wanted. She's already halfway running the place, and the doctor's learned to dodge her. She's determined to be home in time for Torey's wedding. They argued with her to start with, but she wasn't having it. She's made it clear that she plans to be there no matter what, and she's got that doctor of hers on a short leash."

Cara smiled. "That sounds like Ruby."

"Speaking of Torey's wedding…" Nick hesitated. "I wondered if maybe we could talk about that."

Her heart thudded. That didn't sound good. "All right."

"Not here. Too much chance of interruption. Are you done? Anything I could help you finish up?" When she shook her head, he went on, "Then are you game to take a walk?"

"All right." She took off her apron and set it on the counter. "Where?"

Nick thought for a second. "There's nobody down by the lake right now. We'll walk that way."

But she noticed that when they left the dining hall, he didn't take the more well-traveled path leading toward Bluejay Lake but veered sideways onto a trail leading toward the back side of the water.

He really was trying to avoid people today. Whatever he wanted to talk about, he didn't want to be interrupted.

Her heart pounded as they walked, and she sneaked quick glances up at him, trying to guess which way this conversation was going to go. His jaw was set, and he had a do-or-die look on his face. He wasn't talking. He also wasn't holding her hand.

A chilly lump formed in her stomach. Obviously, he'd thought better of the direction their friendship had taken when he was stressed out about Ruby, and now he had to break that news to her. This conversation wasn't likely to be very pleasant, and suddenly she just wanted it over with. So as soon as the lake glinted through the trees, she stopped walking.

"This is far enough," she said. "We can talk here as well as anyplace else."

He glanced around them and nodded. "All right." He took a breath. "Look, Cara. I don't know exactly how to say this, but about us going together to Torey's wedding… I'd like to…uh…change that plan."

"You want to cancel? That's fine." She was proud of how steady her voice sounded. "Don't worry about it for a minute. You have a lot going on, and it's a really emotional time for your family. I completely understand."

He studied her, and one corner of his mouth twitched upward in a half smile. "No," he said slowly, "I don't think you do."

Then he leaned down and kissed her.

Chapter Twelve

Nick kept the kiss gentle and short. When he lifted his head to gauge Cara's reaction, his heart was in his throat.

That had been a bold move—and a desperate one. Not the first bold, desperate move he'd made in his life. He was no stranger to high-stakes situations, although oddly enough, kissing Cara felt more dangerous than most of the others.

But he'd risked it because he needed to know if she was feeling the same way he was. He couldn't tell yet, but she hadn't pulled away. That was something.

She looked up at him, her face blank with surprise, her eyes full of questions. For some women that kiss might have explained everything, but not Cara. She'd want this all spelled out. He'd better start talking.

He cleared his throat. "I still want us to go to Torey's wedding together. But not as friends."

She raised her eyebrows. "I'm…getting that."

He waited, but she didn't protest. So far, so good.

Explaining the rest of it would be harder—partly because he still didn't fully understand it himself, but he'd give it his best shot.

"I've started to…care about you, Cara. And the boys," he added, because it was true, and because she needed to know that he understood that they were part of this. "This thing…you and me… It may have started out as a friendship, but it's getting to be more than that. For me anyway."

"More than friendship," she repeated softly. That little worry line puckered between her brows. "Nick, you have so much going on right now with Ruby and your family. Are you sure that this isn't just..."

She left the sentence unfinished, but he could read between the lines. She was suggesting that maybe the two things were connected, his concern about Ruby and this change in his feelings. He started to deny it, to assure her that the two situations had nothing to do with each other.

But then he stopped. Because, he realized, maybe they did, and whatever this turned out to be, he wasn't going to start it by telling her anything less than the truth.

"I don't know," he said. "It's sure brought home to me how important family is. So, yeah, that may be part of it. But it's not all of it," he went on. Because that was also the truth. "I'd been feeling...different...about you before. It's one of the reasons I put in for the park ranger job. Remember? I told you."

"I remember. But—" She looked up at him, her brow crinkled. "Nick, you've never wanted to stay anyplace very long. And I can't..." She stopped, looking uncomfortable. "I don't know exactly how to put this."

He didn't like the sound of that. "Just say it."

"I can't date just for the fun of it," she said. "Especially not a man with no intention of being here for the long haul. I have the boys to think about, but it's not only that. I have myself to think about, too. I don't want to...invest in something that I know from the beginning can't last. I know what you said about long-distance relationships, how you can care about people even when you're far away from them. But that's friendships, mostly. Even with your sisters and brothers and Ruby, it's...different than this would be. Isn't it?"

"Yeah, it is." He took her hands in his. In spite of the

warmth of the summer morning, they felt chilly, and he rubbed them gently. "That's what I'm trying to tell you, Cara, and not doing such a good job of. This—the way I'm starting to feel about you—this is different."

"You said that already. But what does that mean?"

"I don't know yet," he admitted honestly. "All I know is that I want to figure it out. I guess what I'm asking is if you're willing to figure it out with me."

She made him wait for her answer, as she thought it through in her careful way. Finally, just when he thought he couldn't take it another minute, she nodded.

"I think so," she said. "I've been…feeling differently about you, too, lately."

His heart jumped and he squeezed her hands. "Cara—"

"But I'm not sure it matters. The kind of relationship I can be a part of… It really doesn't sound like something you do, Nick."

"It's not something I've done," he corrected gently. "There's a difference."

She studied him, and in her green eyes he thought—he wasn't sure, but he thought—he saw the stirrings of hope. "Maybe," she admitted cautiously. "Maybe there is."

That was all she said. She hadn't really answered his question, but he decided to stop while he was ahead. She hadn't slammed the door in his face. That was good enough for now.

And she held his hand all the way back up the trail until they parted ways at the dining hall. That was even better.

He was on Ruby duty that evening, so as soon as he left the camp, he pointed his truck south toward Atlanta. They were taking turns popping into the rehab ward of the hospital. So far they were happy about the progress their mom was making, but they intended to keep a very close eye on things, just the same.

When he came into Ruby's room, a young, blonde nurse was just getting her settled back into bed. The nurse glanced up at him and smiled.

"Perfect timing," she said. "We just got back from her physical therapy session."

"How'd it go?" He approached the bed and leaned down to kiss the top of Ruby's head. She reached up and patted his cheek with one age-spotted hand.

"Hannah, honey, this here's my son Nick. My last *single* son," she added. "Just about as eligible as they come, and he's got the best heart in the world. And ain't he fun to look at?"

Hannah laughed, offered Nick a shy, hopeful smile. "Nice to meet you."

"You, too." He kept his own smile polite but brief. "I hope Ruby's behaving herself."

"Oh, she is."

Nick looked at his foster mom, who winked at him saucily. "Somehow I doubt that."

"Oh, no. She's wonderful," Hannah said. "Everybody loves her."

"That," Nick said, "I don't doubt." He dropped into a chair and held his mom's hand as Hannah fluttered around for a few more minutes, then left the room.

"She's a good nurse, that one," Ruby said. "Just broke up with her boyfriend, which, if you ask me, ain't such a bad thing. He sounds like a skunk. Sweet, pretty girl like that won't stay unattached for long, though." She shot Nick a speculative look. "And she might make good sense for you, what with all those dangerous stunts you keep pulling. Might not hurt to have a nurse in the family. She likes traveling, too. I asked."

Nick hesitated. He hadn't planned to talk about this thing with Cara, but maybe he should. "About that—" he said.

"Ah." His mom shot him a sharp look. "So, that's how it is. You've taken yourself off the market. Cara's the reason for that, I'm guessing?"

For a second he was too surprised to answer. "How on earth did you know?"

"I heard about her showing up at the hospital when I had my surgery. Besides," she added, swatting his arm, "I told you I didn't think it was a good idea, you going after Cara. If that's not a way to make a man look twice at a woman, I don't know what is. And no," she went on. "Before you ask, this was no plan of mine. I meant what I said about the two of you needing different things. I still ain't sure how you're planning to work that part out."

"I put in for the park ranger job at Red Hawk."

"Heard about that, too."

He waited, but she didn't say anything else. "I have to say I thought you'd be happier to hear that news."

Ruby sighed. "It just don't seem like your sort of job. You'll spend a lot of time outdoors—that part'll suit you. But Red Hawk's such a dinky little place. Most you'll ever deal with will be litterers, maybe a few out-of-season hunters in the fall. Not near as exciting as what you're used to. My guess is you'll be bored out of your mind by Christmas. But I reckon you know that already."

He did know that. So he shifted in his chair and didn't say anything.

Ruby studied him through smudged bifocals. Finally she sighed and shook her head. "Well, could be I was wrong. I'd always figured God would give you a wife who'd want to travel with you. Instead, maybe He'll give you a heart to stay home." She didn't sound too certain of it.

And a wife? His heartbeat skittered sideways at the thought. "It's a little early to be talking about marriage, Ruby."

"Is it?" She lifted one skimpy gray eyebrow. "If a rolling stone like you is thinking about taking a permanent job Stateside, I'm not so sure. Besides, Cara's got three little boys to raise. You want her to take you seriously, you'll have to put some roots down right quick. That's going to be a mighty big change for you," his mother pointed out. "Ain't it?"

Another nurse came in then, so Nick was saved from having to answer. Honestly, he wasn't sure what to say.

He knew—and that kiss had only made him more certain—that his new feelings for Cara were something special. But he wasn't sure yet where all this was going, and Ruby's mention of marriage had his stomach twisted into a knot.

He knew she was right. The road he'd have to take to pursue a relationship with Cara wasn't one he'd been down before. And while he'd never shied away from new experiences, this was different.

This wasn't just about him.

If he messed this up, if he misjudged himself or these feelings, he'd hurt four people who'd already been hurt far too much.

And apparently Ruby—who knew him better than anybody—had the same concerns Cara did.

The kind of relationship I can be a part of doesn't sound like something you do, Nick.

Cara's words echoed in his memory. He glanced out the hospital window just in time to see a jet soaring skyward after a recent departure from the Atlanta airport. He watched it, remembering the feel of takeoff, the energizing excitement of a fresh trip and a new adventure.

Ruby caught him looking. "Wondering where it's going?" she murmured as the nurse checked her blood pressure. "Or wishing you was on it?"

"A little of both, I guess."

Her hazel eyes met his, kind and concerned. "You know I'm behind you, whatever you do. But you'd better be sure about this, son, before you take it much farther. Really, really sure."

Then she sighed again and gave his hand a squeeze.

The next afternoon, Cara carried a cardboard box of industrial-size cookie sheets and other baking tools into Angelo's, returning the items Maggie had loaned her. The triplets tagged behind, grubby and tired from another busy day at camp. They perked up, though, when Maggie offered them complimentary cookies and milk.

"Sit right here at our best table," Maggie said with a smile, settling them at a spot near the counter. "Angelo will keep an eye on them," she murmured to Cara. "I'd like to talk to you in the kitchen."

"Okay," Cara said. "Be good," she warned the boys, shooting an apologetic look at Angelo, the co-owner of the eatery. "Thanks," she said awkwardly.

The balding man glanced up from the pastries he was arranging in the display case and shrugged. "You're welcome. But fair warning. If they give me any trouble, I'm making them each an espresso and sending 'em home with you."

Maggie made a face at him. "Don't pay any attention to Angelo. He talks tough, but he's a big softie. You watch. He'll sneak them each another cookie as soon as we're out of sight. Come on, let's go put this stuff up."

Cara carried the box into the kitchen, wondering what Maggie wanted to talk about. Had word somehow gotten out that she and Nick were… She didn't know quite what to call it yet.

She hoped Maggie wouldn't ask her questions because she sure didn't have any answers. She'd barely seen Nick since their walk to the lake—and that unexpected, heart-stopping kiss. She'd relived that moment, and the conversation after it, a thousand times since then.

She still hadn't figured it all out. She only knew that when she thought about Nick, her heart jumped, and she couldn't help smiling.

"Thanks for returning these so fast," Maggie said.

"Thank you for loaning them. They made cooking at the camp a lot easier. I kept the muffin tins, though. I plan to use them on the last day, but I'll bring them back right after."

"That's fine." Maggie nodded. "Hard to believe camp's almost over. What with all the preparations for Torey's wedding and then Ruby scaring us half to death, this summer has flown by. Between family stuff and Angelo's, I've been so busy that my shirttail hasn't touched my back in weeks."

"Anything I could help with?" Cara offered tentatively.

Maggie gave her a quick, sideways look. "Funny you should ask. That's what I wanted to talk to you about. Now that camp's winding up, would you be interested in working part-time here at the bakery?"

"Oh!" This was a surprise. "I…don't know."

"Nick said you already have a job lined up for fall." Maggie started unpacking the box. "But I was impressed by what I saw of your cooking up at the camp, and we could really use an extra pair of hands around here. I know you have three kids to take care of, so I'm willing to work with you on scheduling. Even if you could only help out a few hours on weekends, or when we have a catering job, it'd be great."

Cara thought it over. Cooking alongside someone like Maggie? That was awfully tempting. "I think I'd like that. I couldn't do too many hours, though, because I wouldn't feel right asking my dad to babysit too often."

"Wonderful!" Maggie clapped her hands and gave Cara a quick hug. "You can start the Saturday after the wedding at seven a.m. And I understand about your dad. Just stay as long as you feel comfortable."

"I'll be here," Cara promised, her heart pounding. Her father probably wouldn't be too happy, but she didn't see the harm. Helping out here wouldn't interfere with her teaching job, and she'd still get to work with food, at least on the weekends.

It did seem like the perfect solution. And Nick, she was sure, would approve.

At the thought of Nick, an idea occurred to her.

"Maggie? Was this—you hiring me to work here—was that Nick's idea?"

"What? No. I've barely seen Nick lately. We're doing shifts with Ruby, so we're rarely in the same place at the same time. Like I said, with Torey's wedding coming up, and all the trips to Atlanta, we're spread pretty thin these days. Speaking of Nick, though." Maggie turned, leaning one hip against the counter as she faced Cara. "I wanted to ask you something."

Here it came. Cara braced herself. "What?"

"Has Nick said anything to you about taking the job as the Red Hawk park ranger? Permanently, I mean?"

"He mentioned it," Cara admitted cautiously.

"Did he tell you why he wanted the job?"

She wasn't sure what to say, so she hedged. "Why do you ask?"

"It's just so out of character for him, looking into a job like that. Logan said he was dumbfounded when Nick called to ask about it."

"But it's a park ranger job. Isn't that the kind of thing he likes?"

"For a summer? Sure. But for the long haul? No. Nick

doesn't do long-term things. He's addicted to change. Well," she amended with a wry laugh, "that and adrenaline. Being the ranger of a little park in the middle of nowhere, Georgia? That's not Nick. Logan asked why he was interested in sticking around, but Nick sidestepped his questions. Although," Maggie went on, "I have a pretty good idea what this is about. Or, more specifically, *who*."

Cara's pulse pounded in her ears. "Oh?"

"It's Ruby."

"Ruby?"

"He's worried about her. It's the only thing that makes sense. Nick's that way. He doesn't make a show of it, but when he cares about a person, he'll do whatever it takes to help them." She shook her head. "I think it's because of his mom. She was sick for a long time when he was a kid. He wasn't like the rest of us. He had a parent who loved him before he came to Ruby's." Maggie spoke matter-of-factly and without a trace of self-pity. "Losing her was really hard on him."

"I didn't know that." Come to think of it, there must be a lot she didn't know about Nick.

"He doesn't talk about her much. But I think that Ruby being so sick flipped some sort of switch. He feels like he needs to stay closer to home now." Maggie shook her head.

Cara studied her expression. "You don't think that's a good thing?"

The other woman sighed. "I wish I did. It'd be wonderful to have him close by. But Nick's never been a stay-at-home kind of guy. He was telling us a few weeks ago about this medical clinic in El Salvador. They've been after him to head up that building project, and he was planning on it. Nick's great at what he does," Maggie said proudly. "You wouldn't believe the good he's done all around the world."

Cara's heart settled heavily in the bottom of her chest.

The fragile hopes she'd been entertaining since Nick's kiss were popping like soap bubbles.

Because Maggie was right.

Nick wasn't a stay-at-home kind of guy. He might try to be. He might even want to be. But he wasn't. It was as simple as that. And thanks to her disastrous marriage, she knew what happened when a man was forced to try to be something he wasn't.

It didn't work out well.

Angelo stuck his head into the kitchen. "You'd better come out here," he said to Cara. "Your kids need you."

"Coming!" She was torn between relief at an excuse to end this conversation with Maggie and concern about what her sons had gotten into.

"You better come, too," Angelo said to Maggie. "Some of this trouble's got your name on it."

Cara hurried out of the kitchen and stopped short in the doorway.

Her boys were seated where she'd left them—but they weren't alone. Nick sat beside them, showing them how to blow into straws to shoot their paper covers at each other. There was an incriminating litter of empty straw papers around their table.

"Deal with that brother of yours," Angelo muttered to Maggie as he turned back to the display case. "He's making a mess."

"Nick," Maggie spluttered. "For pity's sake! You're being a bad influence and you're wasting straws."

"Sorry, sis. I'll pay for them." Her brother grinned at her. "Hi, Cara." As his eyes met hers, the grin faded, and his expression gentled and warmed.

"Hi." The one word was all she could manage. Her knees had gone weak, and every rational thought had fled her mind. Just one look from this guy, and she'd been whisked right back to the lake and the moment of their kiss.

She could feel her cheeks stinging pink. Nick studied her, and now there was something odd in his face—a wary uncertainty.

Nick had never seemed unsure about anything before.

Cara's stomach did a series of nervous somersaults.

Fortunately, Maggie had stooped to pick up the straw papers off the floor, and she didn't notice. Cara belatedly hurried to help.

"Boys, no more blowing straws," she scolded as she gathered the spent papers. "You know better."

"Don't blame them," Maggie said with a snort. "My brother forgets he's supposed to be a grown-up. Angelo, why on earth didn't you just tell him to stop?"

"Because! You're always telling me to be nice! So, I was nice!" Angelo threw up his hands and disappeared into the kitchen, muttering. "But fine. Next time when things go wrong, I yell."

"Not what I meant, Angelo!" Maggie sounded exasperated. Nick chuckled as he watched his sister trail Angelo into the kitchen, and Cara caught herself staring.

Sitting there, all relaxed and smiling again, Nick was... really good-looking. And then there was the way her boys were gazing up at him, hero worship shining plainly in their eyes.

But there'd been no mistaking that odd uneasiness before when their eyes had met. And Maggie's words echoed in her memory.

Nick doesn't do long-term things. He's never been a stay-at-home kind of guy.

Cara sighed and felt a sudden sympathy for Angelo.

Right now she felt like yelling, too.

Chapter Thirteen

"I see you hiding there." Cara spoke sternly into the almost-empty pantry. "You have to move. That last can of corn belongs in the giveaway box with the rest of the leftovers."

The lizard's green head darted out beside the can, and he looked in her direction with beady eyes. She shuddered.

She didn't care what Nick or her sons said. Lizards were icky.

"Shoo," she said. "Scuttle off to some other hidey-hole for the rest of the day. Tomorrow this whole place will be yours, and you can slither wherever you like."

That didn't make her feel very cheerful, but it was true. Today was the last day of camp, and she'd just finished cleaning up after lunch. Tonight she'd come back for the bonfire and parent assembly. She'd expected to handle the campfire food, but the sheriff's office was taking care of that, leaving nothing for her to do.

"My deputies will bring the hot dogs and grill them," Logan had said. "We'll add some chips, pickles, sodas and iced tea, and let that do it. We're keeping it simple. Nick and I have Torey's rehearsal dinner tonight, so we can't be here, but I'll have half a dozen officers on-site to do the cooking and handle the bonfire. Nothing for you to worry about at all."

"I'm happy to help," she'd said tentatively. "I could make dessert." She'd been collecting recipes, and she had several contenders she thought the kids and their parents would love.

Logan had waved aside her offer with a smile. "We're just letting the kids toast marshmallows for s'mores. You've done us a big favor, Cara, stepping in as cook at the last minute, but you're one of our camp parents, too. I want you to enjoy tonight with your boys."

She'd smiled and thanked him, but she'd really rather have been in charge of the food. She'd have loved the opportunity to fix one more meal for her campers, and she'd have done something a lot fancier than hot dogs and chips.

But Logan was being very considerate. She appreciated his thoughtfulness, especially since his whole family was still focused on Ruby. Now that she'd bullied her doctor into allowing her to go home early, her foster kids' efforts had shifted to keeping their convalescing mother from overdoing.

From what she'd heard, that was proving to be a full-time job. She'd barely seen Nick since he'd shown up at Angelo's.

She wasn't so sure that was a bad thing, though. She'd needed time to think over what Maggie had said—and to face what that uncharacteristic wariness in Nick's eyes meant.

"Hi!"

She whirled around to find Nick behind her. He was wearing his uniform, and he was smiling—a real smile that reached his eyes. He hadn't smiled quite like that since Ruby had taken sick.

In spite of the doubts in her heart, seeing him happy again made her smile, too.

"Nick! I didn't expect to see you today."

"I hated to miss the last day. We can't come tonight because of the wedding stuff, so I dropped by to say goodbye to the kids. And I needed to touch base with you about tomorrow. I'd planned to pick you up, but apparently I have to be at the church early for pictures." He made a face. "I wasn't sure you'd want to sit through all that."

Her stomach fell. So much for their date.

"That's fine. I'll just drive myself." Better that way, she told herself firmly. Probably a good idea to start putting a little distance between them.

Nick's smile faded, but he nodded. "Can't say I blame you. What are you doing?"

"Emptying the pantry. We're putting all the leftovers in a box so that the parents can help themselves to whatever they'd like. Anything they don't take we'll donate to a food pantry."

"Good plan."

"But your blue-tailed friend is holding the last can of corn hostage."

"Is he?" Nick stepped past her to retrieve the can. The tiny lizard scurried off indignantly, his sapphire tail wagging behind him.

"Good riddance!" Cara called after him.

Nick laughed. "Admit it. You're going to miss him."

"I most definitely am not." She sighed and looked around the empty pantry. "But there are a lot of things I will miss."

"Like seeing me every morning for coffee." Nick spoke the words lightly, but something in his tone made her heart speed up. "I'm sure going to miss that. I'll be working up here all by my lonesome after today."

"You've definitely got the job, then?"

"It's mine if I want it." Nick followed her out of the pantry and waited as she stowed the corn in the box with the other leftovers.

"And do you? Want the job?"

He'd been looking out the windows at the view, but he glanced back at her then. He studied her for a second, that odd uncertainty back in his eyes. "Well," he pointed out quietly. "I applied for it."

"I know." She fiddled with a perfectly folded dishcloth. "But Maggie mentioned something about another job, building a medical clinic in El Salvador."

If she hadn't been watching him closely, she might have missed it—the regret that flickered across his face before he firmed up his jaw and answered her.

"Yeah, I turned that down."

"Did you?" She folded and refolded the dish towel. "It sounded…like your kind of thing."

There was a short silence. She could feel Nick watching her, but she kept her eyes down.

"It would've been a few months ago, maybe. Now I've got other plans."

"You don't think you'll be sorry later? That you didn't go?"

"Cara?" When he said her name, she looked up. That was a mistake. Their eyes caught and held, and her stomach promptly started doing somersaults. "I've tried to be honest with you about how I'm feeling about…everything. Maybe you should do the same. Do you *want* me to go to El Salvador?"

She stared back at him helplessly. There was only one truthful answer to that question. "No. No, I don't."

"Okay." He held her gaze a second longer then glanced at his watch. "I feel like we should talk about this more, but I need to get going. See you tomorrow night?"

"I'll meet you at the church."

"Good." He flashed her a smile and was out the door before it registered that he hadn't answered her question—about whether he'd be sorry later that he hadn't gone to build the clinic. She was pretty sure she knew why.

Because there was only one truthful answer to that question, too.

She bit her lip hard, wadded the dish towel up and chucked it into the sink.

Saturday evening, Nick breathed a sigh of relief as the music for the recessional swelled through the sanctuary. Torey and Patrick had been married in Cedar Ridge Christian Church in a solemn, beautiful ceremony with their soon-to-be-adopted kids, Josh and Jill, looking on. Ruby had balked at being rolled down the aisle in a wheelchair, but she'd managed to walk to her seat safely, supported by Nick. They were all watching her like a hawk, but so far she seemed to be holding up great.

Everything had gone perfectly, and once he'd escorted his sister Jina back up the aisle, his duties as a groomsman would be over. Then he'd find a quiet corner and pull Cara aside so they could finish the conversation they'd started back at the camp.

He'd thought of little else since he'd left her in the dining hall.

When he'd asked her if she wanted him to go to El Salvador, his heart had been in his throat. And when she'd said she didn't, the relief that had rushed through him had been mixed with something else, something new.

A rock-solid certainty.

He wasn't sure yet how everything was going to work out, but he was sure now of one very important thing. The life he wanted—the only future he could imagine worth having—included Cara and the boys.

That much was settled—on his end, anyway. He'd do whatever it took, make any sacrifice, to have them in his life long term. There was no longer any question about that.

The only question was whether she'd be willing to do the same.

At the moment, she was sitting in a pew alone, wearing a sea-colored dress that intensified the green in her eyes. Earlier, when he'd caught her eye and winked, her answering smile had seemed forced.

He wondered if the unsettled feelings between them were bothering her as much as they were bothering him. Or maybe being at a wedding had stirred up old hurts. The idea that he'd caused Cara pain by inviting her here worried him, and probably meant this wasn't the best time for them to talk.

He hated the idea of waiting. He'd already been held hostage for hours by wedding stuff. He'd endured rehearsals, endless picture taking and various minor mishaps, all with his mind fixed on Cara. His patience was nearing its breaking point.

There were things he needed to say—important things. Ruby was right. He had to be clear with Cara that he was serious about this, about her. And the sooner the better.

On the other hand, he really didn't want to mess this up. If he needed to wait, he'd wait.

But it wouldn't be easy.

When Torey and Patrick had swept back down the aisle, and he'd safely turned Jina back over to her husband, he detoured by Ruby to offer his help getting her to the reception. She waved him off with a twinkle in her eye.

"I got more folks fussing over me than I can handle. You go see about Cara. Logan and Ryder can look after me."

She had a point. His brothers were already closing in. Ruby was in good hands. He grinned and leaned to kiss her cheek. She flapped a hand at him.

"Scat."

He caught up with Cara just outside the church door.

"Hi," he said.

She turned—and took his breath away. She was even prettier up close. "You look…" Words failed him. "Beautiful," he ended lamely.

He wished he could have thought of a better word. *Beautiful* didn't begin to cover it.

Cara was beautiful wearing shorts and an oversize apron, with her hair tied back in a kerchief. But today, all prettied up for a wedding?

She looked amazing.

Her short-sleeved blue-green dress was simply cut, and he liked the way it fluttered around her, rippling like waves on a tropical beach. Her hair was caught up and pinned in place with a jeweled clasp shaped like a hummingbird. Little tendrils escaped to frame her face, and although she was wearing a touch more makeup than usual, she'd kept it light and natural.

He liked that, too. And he especially liked that he could still see that summer sprinkle of freckles across her nose.

"Thanks," she was saying. "You look pretty nice yourself."

He hated suits. But the shy admiration in her voice made this one worth it.

"They've done the photos, so I can head to the reception now." That was being held in a brick depot constructed centuries ago. Now that the trains it served had vanished, the weathered building was a popular local spot for fancy events. "Want to ride together?"

"Oh!" Cara looked uncertain. "Thanks, but I'd better drive my own car. I left the boys with my dad, and I wouldn't want you to have to leave early if something came up."

Her objection was sensible, but that didn't make Nick

like it any better. "Hopefully nothing will come up, but if it does, I wouldn't mind leaving early."

She shook her head. "I wouldn't feel right about making you miss any part of tonight. It'll be easier to drive separately."

Again, sensible and right. Just not what he wanted to hear. "All right, then. I'll see you there."

She nodded and smiled—sort of. There still seemed something off. He watched her hurry toward the parking lot, thinking.

He didn't like this. His instincts, the instincts that had saved his bacon more than once, prickled, telling him that something was wrong. He weighed his options as people milled around him, reclaiming their vehicles to make the short drive over to the depot.

By the time he'd walked to his own truck, he'd come to a decision.

He'd talk to Cara now, tonight. Maybe it wasn't the best time or place for it, but he sensed that—for some reason—time was running out.

He'd never liked sitting around and waiting for trouble. He'd always preferred to meet it head-on, on his own terms. So, that's what he'd do.

Maybe an honest talk would clear the air between them, sweeping away the confusion and uncertainty and setting the first stones of that sturdy foundation he wanted to build.

Maybe it would put an end to everything he was hoping for.

Either way, he was about to find out.

Chapter Fourteen

The old depot had been transformed into a wonderland of twinkling lights, flickering candles and white gauzy drapes. Creamy magnolia blossoms and their glossy green leaves spilled over the white tablecloths, and Maggie's towering cake, festooned with flowers and leaves, occupied the place of honor. Nick had seen it all before, when they'd come here for the photos, and though he was no expert on wedding decorations, overall he approved. It looked classy and simple at the same time, perfect for his no-frills sister.

The arriving guests approved, too because there was a lot of oohing and aahing as people walked in. He kept having to dodge people who stopped to admire this little touch or that one. Most of them wanted to talk to him, too, which made things even more difficult. He didn't want to be rude, but he needed to find Cara. Her car was parked outside, so she was here someplace.

He poked his head into the kitchen area, thinking maybe she'd been unable to resist helping with the food prep. Cara was nowhere to be seen, but his sister Maggie was there, her bridesmaid's dress swathed in a huge apron, busy as a bee.

"Have you seen Cara?" he asked.

"She stuck her head in a minute ago and asked if I needed any help. I told her we had it under control. Can't risk getting anything on that pretty dress of hers. I think she went out back," Maggie said. "But I wasn't really paying attention. Sorry, I've got to get the buffet set up."

"No, you don't." Angelo carried in a stack of metal containers, his big hands muffled in bright red oven mitts and his expression thunderous. "What you got to do is go out there and have yourself a good time. Celebrate with your family. I got this. Take off that apron and get outta my way."

"No. There's too much to do," Maggie said. As Nick walked out the back door, an argument ensued, with Angelo bellowing and Maggie ignoring him.

Behind the depot was a courtyard, also strung with lights. The building perched on a hill, overlooking the town below, which was beginning to twinkle in the dusk of the day. It was pretty, but they wouldn't get much use out of this space tonight. He smelled rain in the air, and his shoulder was aching. Unless he missed his guess, there'd be a downpour soon.

Cara stood at the far end of the grassy rectangle, arms crossed in front of her body, looking at the view. She turned as he approached.

"I've been looking for you," he said.

"I was just…getting a breath of air."

Nick raised his eyebrows. It was early August in Georgia. The air in the courtyard could have come straight out of one of Angelo's ovens.

"I'm sorry, Cara. I should have realized that weddings might not be your thing."

"What? Oh. Because of how my own marriage turned out." She shook her head. "Not at all. It makes me happy to see couples so much in love, like Torey and Patrick tonight. A little…wistful, maybe. But mostly happy. I like knowing that everybody's story doesn't end like mine, that there are still happily-ever-afters in the world."

"Good." He took a breath. Thanks to the heat and the brewing rainstorm, people were staying inside, and the courtyard was still deserted. This was as good a time as any to spell out his feelings. “Because I’m thinking maybe we should try for one of those ourselves.” She looked up sharply but didn’t speak, so he added, “A happily-ever-after. You and me.”

She took a quick, broken breath. “Oh, Nick.”

There were a dozen ways she could have said his name which would have made him the happiest man alive. That wasn’t one of them.

Then again, maybe she didn’t understand what he meant.

“I’m not trying to rush you into anything. I just want you to know that I’m serious about this—about you. About the boys. I want you to know that I’m willing to do whatever it takes to make this work for you.”

“To make it work,” she repeated, a funny note in her voice. “For me.”

“That’s right. To make it work for you and for the boys.”

She tilted her head and looked at him. Even in the dimming light, he could see that her eyes were sad.

“You don’t believe me,” he said.

“I believe you, Nick. You’d try to fit yourself into a life that worked for me and for the boys. The problem is…”

“What?”

“I just don’t see any way that life would work for you.”

Nick was frowning at her.

“I don’t understand.”

She swallowed hard. “The life you’re describing. There’s just no way it would work for you.”

His frown deepened. “What part?”

“Any of it. The park ranger job, living here in Cedar Ridge—or any place, for that matter—full-time.” *Having an instant family of three little boys.* She didn’t say that out loud. He hadn’t talked about marriage specifically yet, only hinted. “That’s a huge lifestyle change, Nick.”

"That doesn't matter. I'll make it work. Cara, I still don't think you understand what I'm getting at." He paused, his dark eyes searching hers with an intensity she felt all the way to her toes. "I'm trying to tell you I'm falling in love with you."

Her heart melted, not just at the words, but at the raw honesty in his voice. He meant what he was saying. Or he thought he did.

And he was waiting for her answer.

I'm falling in love with you, too. She wanted to tell him that, more than anything. It was true. She'd been falling for Nick for so long that she couldn't remember when it had started.

Maybe the first time he'd complimented her cooking. Or when he'd offered her the job at the camp, making her feel as if she was something special, for the first time in eons. Or when he'd given that job back to her, after finding her crying in the pantry. When she'd seen how kind and gentle he was with her sons. When he'd shown her the fawn.

When he'd kissed her.

She wasn't sure. Her feelings had grown so naturally that she couldn't trace them back to a starting point.

But telling him that now would only complicate things. This feeling with Nick… Maybe it felt like the first time she'd ever fallen in love, but it wasn't. She had to keep reminding herself of that. She'd been down this road before, and she knew what could happen, especially when a man tried to live a life he wasn't suited for.

She'd thought this through. She knew what she had to say, although she hadn't planned on saying it all tonight. His sister's wedding seemed like an awful time to have this conversation, but Nick hadn't given her any choice.

"Love isn't always enough." It took every ounce of her willpower to say those words. "Not when two people are as different as we are. Falling in love is easy. Staying in love, that's the hard part. Todd fell in love with me, too, back at the beginning, and I fell for him. I knew he liked an easy life, liked to have fun. I was so serious, and he was always the life of the party. I thought that was a good thing, that we balanced each other out. But when the triplets were born, everything changed. Todd…couldn't adapt."

"He should have. You did."

"It was different for me. I'm not sure Todd was capable of it. Even one baby would have been too much for him, but three, with medical problems…" She shook her head. "It was too much. He hated dealing with all that. That's why he…did what he did. He's not a horrible man. He just wanted to stop being miserable."

He shook his head. "You're a lot kinder than I am."

"I wasn't at first. It was bad enough that he abandoned me, but turning his back on the boys… That was a harder thing for me to forgive." She took a deep breath. "It took a lot of prayer for me to get to the point where I didn't hate him. And I just can't… I just can't go through all that again."

"I see." Nick said slowly. He looked as if she'd slapped him. "If after all the time we've spent together you can believe I'm anything, *anything* like that guy, then you're right. There's no point in us having this conversation."

She was hurting him and making him mad, and she hated that.

"No," she said gently. "You're not like Todd. You're stronger than he was, and I don't think you'd have done what he did, not in a million years. I guess I'm not saying this very well. It's just that I learned something, going through all that with him. I learned that we can't…" She struggled for the right way to put this. "We can't change who we are for somebody else, no matter how much we care about them. And, Nick, you're not the kind of guy who lives in the suburbs, works a nine-to-five job and worries about weeds in his lawn or whether the dishwasher is draining right. You're just…not."

"Maybe I haven't been." He ran one hand roughly through his hair. "But I can do those things, Cara. I'm willing to do those things."

She sighed. "But you'd be miserable, Nick. I think deep down you know it. I'm afraid eventually you'd resent the boys and me for tying you down, and I'd… I'd really hate that."

Her voice wobbled on the last bit. Because she *would* hate that. She'd hate seeing misery and frustration in Nick's face when he looked at her, like a wild animal trying to gnaw his own leg off to escape a trap.

And sooner or later, she would.

For a second he didn't answer. Twilight was upon them now, and the sunlight had faded. But even in the glow of the gentle lights strung in the trees, she could see that his jaw was set, his cheek paler than it should have been.

"Don't tell me what kind of man I am, Cara," he said finally. He spoke quietly but definitely. "It doesn't seem to be a subject you know much about. I'd never resent you or the boys, no matter what happened. I take full responsibility for my own choices." He paused, holding her eyes with his. "Maybe you should, too."

She blinked. "What?"

"I just told you I'm falling in love with you. That I want this…whatever it is…whatever it could be…to work for all of us. And I've promised you that I'll do what it takes to make that happen. That's how I feel. I can't put it any plainer. If you don't feel the same way, you don't have to come up with all of this junk about how miserable you think I'd be. Just tell me the truth."

It was both a demand and a challenge. But she couldn't tell him the truth, because Nick was wrong. She knew a little something about what kind of man he was. If she admitted how she felt about him, he wouldn't hear anything else she had to say.

And if he kissed her again—as he was likely to do—what little willpower she had would dissolve like sugar in tea.

She took a cautious step backward.

"It doesn't matter how I feel."

"As far as I'm concerned, that's the only thing that does matter." Another pause, a deliberate one. She knew what was coming, knew he was giving her time to think about her answer. "How do you feel, Cara? About me? About us?"

She couldn't answer that. Not now. Not honestly. So she stared back at him mutely, her heart pounding as the rising wind rattled the strings of lights draped above them.

"There you are!"

Startled, they both glanced over at the depot. Jina was at the doorway, beckoning to them. "We've been looking for you everywhere! Come on in! Things are getting started."

Before she finished her sentence, Cara was pulling her keys out of her purse. "I'm so sorry," she managed. "I have to go. Something's…come up."

"Cara." Nick pitched his voice low, so Jina wouldn't overhear.

"I'm sorry, Nick." She choked the words out as she headed around the side of the building toward the parking lot.

Her skirt whipped around her as she hurried toward her car. The wind was getting up, and the storm was about to break. She slid onto the seat and tried to think.

She didn't want to go home. Her father and the boys would be surprised to see her back so early, and they'd ask questions.

She didn't want to answer questions, not right now, but she didn't have anyplace else to go. Except…

She could drive to the camp. She still had the key to the gate that she'd been given when she'd started work there. She needed to return it, but she'd forgotten to retrieve Maggie's muffin tins when she'd gone up for the bonfire. She figured she'd get the tins, and then return the key to Nick afterward. She'd meant to go tomorrow, and she'd planned to take them along on her first day working at Angelo's.

Once Nick talked to his sister, Cara doubted the job offer would stand. So, the sooner she got the tins back where they belonged, the better.

Besides, the drive would take a while, and the camp would be deserted. She'd have plenty of time to cry over Nick and all her silly soap-bubble dreams.

Chapter Fifteen

"You sure you don't mind leaving early, Nick?" Ruby looked at him across the truck seat as the windshield wipers thumped a rhythm.

"Not at bit." It was true. He'd been quick to volunteer when Ruby's energy had flagged toward the end of the reception.

He'd drive her home, get her settled for the night. Then he'd retreat to the cabin for some blessed solitude. He was exhausted from pretending to be happy while inside he was agonizing over every word Cara had said.

Or worse, every word she hadn't said.

"Cara didn't stay for dinner. You want to tell me why that was?"

He shifted irritably on the seat. Trust Ruby to pick up on exactly what was bugging him.

"Not really."

"Might help to talk it over."

"I'd better focus on my driving. This storm's getting worse. If I end up in a ditch while you're in my truck, Logan will have my hide."

Ruby snorted. "Peddle that snake oil someplace else. No storm in this world's gonna put you into a ditch. What happened tonight, son?"

He kept his eyes on the road. "Turns out Cara agrees with you. She doesn't think I'm the right guy for her, either." He hated saying that out loud. "Look, this is all too… raw…to paw over tonight." He slowed as the truck splashed through a patch of standing water. "Can't we just drop it? You can tell me 'I told you so' tomorrow just as well."

"What did you just—" Ruby spluttered. "Pull over!"

"What?" He glanced over, alarmed.

She glared back. "Don't you *what* me, Nick Marshall! Stop this truck right this minute."

Thoroughly bewildered, he checked his mirrors and pulled onto the shoulder of the road. "Ruby, what's wrong? Do I need to call an ambulance?" He reached for his phone.

"Put that fool thing away." After unfastening her seat belt, she cupped her hand under his chin and pulled him close until they were nose to nose. "Now you listen to me and listen good. You think I want to *paw* over your hurt feelings? You think I'd *ever* tell you *I told you so* when things have gone bad for you? You ever seen me do it? Tell one of my young 'uns such a thing when their heart was breaking?"

It took him a minute to answer. "No, ma'am. You've never done that."

"I never done that." She repeated the words sternly. "And you should know me better than to think I ever would." She gave his chin a shake, then leaned back in her seat, still staring fiercely at him. "Now, I believe you owe me an apology."

"I owe you a lot more than that." He released his own seat belt and gathered her against his chest, feeling how thin she was now. "I'm sorry, Ruby."

"You're forgiven." She patted his cheek. "It's all right, son. You're hurting, and pain splashes. If you stand close enough to a hurting person, you're bound to get hurt yourself now and again. But part of loving people is hanging on tight when they try to pull away and showing them over and over again that you ain't going anyplace, that they're what matters most to you. Once they come to believe that, all the struggle is worth it, a thousand times over."

As Nick turned her loose, he shot her a look. Ruby began fiddling with her seat belt, unaware how close to home her words had hit.

"You did that for us," he said slowly. "You never gave up, no matter what we said or did."

He hated to think what would've happened if she had.

"Of course not." She shrugged. "I couldn't. You kids, each one of you, you're what mattered most to me."

That was all she said, but he understood. When Ruby loved somebody, she never gave up. They'd all splashed plenty of their hurts on her over the years. Other people in their lives had turned their backs, but not Ruby. She'd responded with an unflinching, plainspoken, matter-of-fact love. Ruby's own particular brand. Social workers had sometimes taken exception to her methods, but Ruby had never wavered, never tried to be anybody other than who she was.

And in the end, she'd been exactly who they'd needed her to be.

"Now drive me home," Ruby said. "This wind's getting wild, and we've both had enough excitement for one day."

They drove the rest of the way in a companionable silence. When they pulled up to her farmhouse, he walked her up the porch steps.

"Want me to stay here with you tonight?"

"Because of this little blow-bluster?" Ruby chuckled. "No, you go on back to the cabin, get yourself some sleep. And don't worry." She gave him a smacking kiss on the cheek. "You'll sort things out. Love always finds its way if you give it time. It's like this rain. When it hits fast, it can cause some damage, be a little scary. But once it sinks in deep, good things can start to grow."

A flicker of hope sparked in his heart as he took her keys and unlocked the door. "Maybe you're right. As usual."

"Well, I seem to have missed the mark a time or two

lately." She winked as she walked inside. "But could be I'm getting back up to speed."

Back at the cabin, he parked his truck and sprinted through the rain to the porch. He paused to look over the view. Tonight it was anything but peaceful. Lightning flashed, thunder rumbled and branches snapped in the wind with earsplitting cracks.

But the storm inside his heart had calmed to a murmur. He wasn't sure what he was going to do, not yet, because whether he liked admitting it or not, Cara wasn't completely wrong in what she'd said.

But like Ruby, he wasn't giving up. Tomorrow he'd start figuring something out.

Although he'd expected a wakeful night, he was asleep not long after his head hit the pillow. He slept like a log until his phone buzzed. He opened an eye and squinted at the display.

The first thing he noticed was the time.

3:00 a.m.

The second thing was the caller's name.

Cara's father.

"Professor Andrews? What's wrong?"

"Is Cara still with you?"

"What? No." Nick scrubbed at his face, trying to rub the sleep out of his eyes. "She left the wedding early. She's not at home?"

"No." The older man's voice shook. "And I can't get her on the phone. I'm really worried."

So was he. Instantly and completely. "I'm on it. Stay by the phone. I'll be in touch when I find her."

When he found her. Not *if. When.*

He kept that thought in his head as he pulled on jeans and a T-shirt. He phoned his brother as he headed out the door.

Logan had been sleeping, too, but he was instantly alert.

"No wrecks with injuries in the county. I'd know. But," he went on grimly, "that doesn't mean she didn't slide off the road someplace. It's been a rough night. I'll alert my deputies and have them drive the routes leading from the depot to her dad's house. If her car's there, we'll find it."

"Good. But she might not have gone straight home. She was…upset when she left."

"Any idea where she might have headed?"

"I don't know." He rubbed his forehead. "The camp maybe? She's still got a key to the gate. I'll drive over and check."

"I'd tell you to stay home and let the professionals take care of this, but I know how much good that would do. Keep me posted, okay?" Logan hung up just as Nick turned over the truck engine.

Nick was glad the rain had slacked off—and that his brother's deputies were busy elsewhere, because he nudged the truck well above the speed limit on the way to the camp. He tried not to think the worst, but it wasn't easy.

This wasn't like Cara. She wouldn't have worried her dad like that, would never have left her boys all night with no notice. Something must have gone really wrong.

His heart fell when he saw the camp gate was closed. He pulled in, preparing to turn around. Then he leaned forward and squinted through the windshield.

The gate was closed, but the padlock was open. Cara was here after all.

Relief warred with fear as he jumped out of the truck to shove the gate wide. The road winding toward the camp was muddy and littered with branches. He saw no tire tracks in the headlight beams, but after the rainfall they'd had, that didn't mean anything.

But if Cara was still here at this hour, without letting

anybody know, something must have happened. He didn't like imagining what he might find.

Part of the mystery was solved about a quarter of a mile below the camp. A tree was down, blocking the road. He inspected the thickness of the trunk. Too big to move without equipment. He killed the engine and grabbed a flashlight and a backpack full of first aid supplies. He'd have to walk the rest of the way.

Slinging the backpack over his shoulder, he aimed the flashlight ahead of him and jogged up the debris-littered road, praying with every sloshy step.

The storm was over. Cara peered out the windows of the dining hall into the darkness. The only sounds she heard were water dripping off the roof and the chorus of frogs down by the lake.

She pressed the button on her watch to illuminate the time and winced. Her poor father must be beside himself by now. She hoped Nick rescued her before the boys got up.

Because she knew—with a certainty that went all the way to her flimsy, high-heeled sandals that made walking any distance impossible—that Nick was coming.

She'd realized that when she'd driven back to the dining hall after finding the road blocked. The storm had been right overhead then, lightning flashing and thunder booming simultaneously. Even the sturdy log walls of the building had shuddered in the force of the wind.

She'd prayed desperately for protection and for peace and for somebody—anybody—to figure out where she was and come help her.

And suddenly an inexplicable peace had washed over her.

Because… Nick.

Sooner or later, Nick would figure out where she was.

And the minute he did, he'd come. Nothing would stop him, not the storm, not that huge fallen tree.

Not even the hurt she'd caused him at the wedding.

He'd find a way to get to her because he was that kind of man. She just had to wait.

Knowing that—believing that—had changed everything.

And so, during the most chaotic night of her life, trapped in a deserted camp while a storm raged around her, her phone broken, the power out, she'd sat in the dining hall—calmly.

She'd prayed for guidance and for courage, and for Nick's safety as he battled his way to her.

And for no lizard to scuttle close in the dark.

And she'd waited.

Behind her the lights in the dining hall flickered back on, and the refrigerator whirred to life. Cara smiled with relief. The storm was officially over. Everything was all right.

Or it would be, once Nick arrived.

An idea occurred to her, and her smile broadened. She picked her way through the twigs and wet leaves to her car. She rummaged in the back seat and returned to the kitchen with one of Maggie's tins, and the gallon baggie of homemade cinnamon muffin mix she'd fixed as a thank-you for the loan of the baking supplies.

She tied on her apron and switched the oven to preheat. Thankfully, there was still some coffee in the canister, so she started that, too, before mixing up the batter.

The coffeemaker had barely started to drip when she heard what she'd been waiting for.

"Cara!" Nick's hoarse shout echoed across the camp.

"In here!" she called, sliding the filled tin into the oven.

He blew through the door so fast he almost knocked it off the hinges, flinging a backpack on the ground as he closed the space between them. Before she knew what was happening, she was gathered into his arms, pressed hard against his chest, and he was murmuring into her hair.

"Thank You, God. Thank You, thank You."

She squeezed her eyes shut and leaned against him, feeling the solid warmth of him under his damp shirt and the rapid beat of his heart under her cheek, smelling the fresh, outdoor smell that clung to him.

They had so much to talk about, to say and to unsay. But all that could wait.

Finally he pulled her gently away and looked down into her face. "Are you all right? Really?"

"I'm fine. I'm so sorry. I drove up here to get Maggie's muffin tins and when I tried to leave there was this tree..."

"I know. I left my truck on the other side of it. But, Cara, nobody could get you on the phone."

She winced. "It's broken. I dropped it in a puddle when I was looking to see if there was any way I could drive around the tree."

Nick fished his own phone out of his pocket. "Call your dad. Then I need to call Logan. He's got half the county looking for you."

Two phone calls, a lot of apologies and explanations later, Nick set the phone on the counter. "Logan's sending somebody to clear the road. It won't take long, and while we wait, you and I need to talk. I've been thinking, and—" He stopped and sniffed. "I smell coffee. And something else." He sniffed again and shot her a disbelieving look. "Cara, for crying out loud. Are you *baking*?"

"Well, I had the muffin tins and a mix I'd made for Maggie, so I—"

That was as far as she got. He stopped her words with a kiss.

He took his time. When he finally lifted his mouth from

hers, she'd completely forgotten what they'd been talking about.

Until he reminded her.

"*Muffins?* I thought I'd find you up here hurt—or worse. At least terrified. But you're baking muffins."

"Yes," she said, looking into his face. He had the nicest eyes. "I thought you might be hungry."

"But how did you know I was coming?"

She couldn't help it. She laughed. "Because I know you." She traced the hard plane of his cheek with her finger. "I know you, Nick," she repeated.

He turned his head to kiss her palm. "You scared me tonight, Cara. And I don't scare easy."

"I'm sorry."

"Don't be. Between this and a talk I had with Ruby, I've realized something. Something important."

"What?"

"What I told you earlier… It wasn't true. I'm not falling in love with you, Cara." Just as her heart stopped beating, he went on. "I'm already in love with you. Before you start arguing, I know you've been hurt, and I understand why you're not sure about me. You're concerned about your kids, and you want to protect them. I get that, and I won't rush you. Take all the time you need, until I've shown you that you can trust me with your heart and with the hearts of those boys. I'll do whatever it takes, Cara. Wait as long as you want me to. I just need one thing from you."

Her heart was so full that she could barely form the words. "What?"

"An answer. You've dodged my question twice. I don't have much to give you, except myself, but I'm yours if you think you could ever learn to care about me. Do you?"

He was holding her hands, and his fingers shook as he asked her the question. That tremble touched her even more than his words, that this man who feared nothing would shake, waiting to know if she could possibly love him.

Could she care for him? What a question. But given how she'd been acting, she supposed she couldn't blame him for not being certain.

Still, turnabout was fair play.

"No," she said softly. The light went out of his eyes, and he started to pull his hands away, but she held on fast. "I can't learn to care about you, Nick, because I already do."

The swift joy that kindled in his eyes almost did her in, but when he leaned close to kiss her again, she shook her head.

"That doesn't mean it'll be easy, Nick. Three boys all at once… It's a lot. And you and I… We're so different."

He smiled. "I've never wanted an easy life. Easy is boring. And sure, we're different, but so what? My sisters and brothers and I are all different, and yeah, that causes problems sometimes, but it doesn't stop us from loving each other."

She thought about his family and smiled. "No, it doesn't."

"Maybe I'm not the kind of guy you'd have picked, Cara. But you know what? I wouldn't have picked Ruby as a foster mom, if I'd been given the choice. She was the right person, just the same. I know I can be the right person for you and the boys. I will be. I promise you that."

She almost laughed again. He sounded so determined.

"You already are, Nick. I wasn't afraid tonight because I knew you were coming, that you'd find a way to get to me. And if it'd been the boys up here, it would have been the same. Wouldn't it?"

"Yeah, it would have." She heard nothing but certainty in his voice.

"I'd been telling myself I couldn't fall for a man who never stayed put, whose life took him all over the world. That I needed somebody steady, somebody I could depend on. And tonight when I was so certain you were coming, when there wasn't a doubt in my mind…well. It finally dawned on me that you're the most dependable man I've ever met. All the traveling, the life you lead, that's just the surface of it, like…" She searched her mind for the right example. "Like water running over a rock. Underneath that you're as steady as granite."

"I'm liking the sound of this," he murmured, leaning in close.

She moved one step back. If he kissed her again now, she'd never say the rest of it. "But, Nick, you have to promise me something."

"Anything."

"Don't take the park ranger job, not because of me. You can't give up the things that make you happy—that make you who you are. I want you to keep traveling, keep having adventures and living the life you love. I just want you to…make some room for me and the boys in it."

He searched her face. "Do you mean that?"

"I do."

The almost-dimple flickered. "I like hearing you say those words. In fact, if I have anything to say about it, you'll be saying them again pretty soon." His smile faded. "But it'll be hard sometimes, Cara, sharing a life like that with me. You sure—really sure—you want to sign up for that?"

She nodded.

He set his jaw. "Then I'll do everything I can to make it easier."

"Just come home to us, Nick. As often as you can."

"Always. And whenever you need me, you or the boys, I'll be there. No matter what."

"I know that," Cara whispered. Because she did.

And this time when he leaned down, she tiptoed to claim the kiss she saw promised in his eyes.

Epilogue

Ruby's farmhouse was full of family. All the windows and doors were open, allowing the cool October breeze to blow through, but the kitchen was still unpleasantly warm.

Nobody cared. They were celebrating Nick and Cara's engagement, and joy was as thick in the air as the aroma of Ruby's fried chicken.

Nick, freshly home from three weeks in El Salvador, stood in a corner, soaking it in. Building the medical clinic had been as rewarding—and as challenging—as he'd expected. And thanks to his new full-time position in Hope for Healing, the organization that built the clinics, he was able to balance his time away with an equal amount of time at home.

So far that seemed to be working pretty well.

Except that he'd missed his family—a lot. He'd never been so homesick before. Of course, it wasn't hard to understand why things were different now. His eyes kept drifting back to Cara, deep in conversation with Maggie.

She was teaching math at the college and doing well. She was also working part-time at Angelo's, planning to transition to full-time once the school year was over. She couldn't wait. Anytime she and Maggie were together, they were discussing Cara's ideas to expand the restaurant's catering services.

Now her green eyes sparkled with excitement, and she gestured enthusiastically, making the emerald on her left hand sparkle. He'd given her that ring the day he'd returned home—and his heart still skipped a beat when he saw it twinkling on her finger.

"Now, then." Ruby walked in, carrying a folded quilt. "Cara, stop talking shop with Maggie, and Nick, come here. I got an early wedding present for you." She set the bundle on the table and sighed. "There it is. The last of my memory quilts. Well, go on," she urged. "Unfold it and take a look."

Nick took one end and Cara the other, and they gently unfolded the large quilt. Soft gasps and murmurs of admiration swelled from the others as the pattern came into view.

A star with both long and short points dominated the center. The border was studded with smaller, simpler stars. The material was a variety of rich colors, mostly blue and green, with exotic touches of purple and gold.

"Ruby," Charlotte, a skilled seamstress herself, spoke with awed admiration. "You've outdone yourself. When you picked out such a difficult pattern, I was worried. But this is beautiful."

"It's called the Mariner's Compass," Ruby explained. "Perfect for our Nick. Every wanderer needs a compass so he can find his way back home."

Logan laughed. "Nick seems to find his way home pretty regularly these days."

"Course he does." Ruby put her arm around Cara's waist. "He's got good reasons to. And see? I built all that in. This star here? I mixed up bits of cloth I got from Nick and Cara to make the middle, and the three points are made from the triplets' clothes. And these bigger points?" She traced the long and short prongs of the center star. "Those came from scarves and shirts and other things Nick sent me from his travels over the years." She pointed to the smaller stars along the border. "I got material from each person in the family, grown-ups and young 'uns alike, and made a star special for each one."

"Look!" Brian pulled his brothers close. "It's our shirts. See? These three right there." He pointed.

"And that next one's mine," Maggie's son Oliver said. "'Cause we're not just friends anymore. We're going to be cousins."

Brian, Scott and Aaron exchanged incredulous looks.

"I didn't even think of that," Scott said.

"We got a real family," Aaron said in an awed voice. "Is Grandpa Andrews there, too?"

"He sure is," Ruby said, pointing to a particularly sedate star.

"Better give me that." Ryder reached for the edge of the quilt Nick was holding. "You've got something else to see to." He nodded at Cara, who was tearing up.

Nick relinquished the quilt and headed to her side. She laughed self-consciously and dabbed her eyes as he pulled her close.

"I'm being silly. It's just all so…much."

"Too much?"

"No." She smiled up at him. "It's perfect, Nick. The quilt. Your family. Us. All of it."

He smiled back. "You'll get no argument out of me."

He was so distracted by Cara that he wasn't sure when Ruby slipped away, but a little while later he noticed she wasn't in the kitchen. He frowned.

"Be right back," he murmured to Cara. "I'm going to check on Ruby." She nodded, tilting her cheek for his kiss.

Such an ordinary thing, something he'd seen his married sisters do a hundred times, but it made his heart stutter. He wondered if he'd ever lose that sense of awe and gratitude he felt whenever Cara took his hand or leaned against his shoulder.

He didn't think he would.

He found Ruby on the porch, gazing over the rolling mountains, rosy and golden in the autumn sunshine.

"Ruby? You feeling okay?"

She smiled. "I'm dandy. Just having myself a little talk with the Lord." She beckoned. "Come here." When he was close enough, she put an arm around his waist. "You all gotta stop worrying over me, Nicky."

"Can't make any promises there."

"Well, it's foolishness. Whether you worry or not, one day—not today, mind, nor any time real soon—I'm gonna pass out of this world. Now, don't look like that." She slapped his arm lightly. "Of all my young 'uns, you're the one who should understand. If you know the Lord, death ain't nothing but the next big adventure. Between you and me, I'm kinda looking forward to it."

"Ruby." The one word was all he could manage.

"Stands to reason, don't it? I ain't ever been anywhere. Hardly ever left Georgia, my whole life. Not like you, with all your wandering. I used to wish I could tag along with you, sometimes. Have myself some adventures, too."

"I'll take you anyplace you want to go. Just say the word."

Ruby shook her head. "No need for that. God's been showing me some things just lately, and—"

Cara pushed the screen door ajar. "Everything all right?"

"Come on out here, honey. You need to hear this, too." Ruby waited until Nick had gathered Cara under his other arm before she spoke again. "You remember me telling you that I didn't think you was the right man for Cara here?" She sighed. "I owe you an apology because it's plain to see I was dead wrong. The truth is, I got too big for my britches, what with my matchmaking working out so well for your brothers and sisters. Started thinking I knew what was best for everybody, and that's poaching on God's property. The good Lord reminded me that He knows exactly what He's doing, and He sure don't need any advice from a silly old woman like me. He's been showing me how short-sighted I was, thinking Nick here couldn't be happy unless he could keep on a-wandering."

"Don't be too hard on yourself," Cara said gently. "I thought the same thing."

Ruby chuckled. "Well, turns out we was both wrong. I shoulda seen it sooner. You ain't got to travel to have yourself an exciting life. Why, a person can have plenty of adventures right at home. Like me. I may not have traveled to foreign parts, but raising my kids? That was an adventure for sure. And I plan to have plenty more adventures with my grand young 'uns before I go to glory." She rested her grizzled gray head against Nick's chest, reaching across to clasp Cara's hand in her age-spotted one. "That's what God's been reminding me about. Loving folks, really loving them, the way He tells us to? There ain't no adventure in this world bigger nor scarier nor better than that!"

"You're a very wise woman, Ruby Sawyer," Nick said solemnly. He was rewarded with a chuckle and a swat.

They stood there together, the three of them, listening to the laughter coming from inside the house and watching the October sun give the clouds a final burst of color and the changing leaves one last, lingering kiss before it sank behind the mountains.

* * * * *

Dear Reader,

I'm so happy you've come along with me on this trip to one of my favorite story towns! Cedar Ridge, Georgia, feels like home to me now—don't you love places like that—whether they're real or imaginary? Places where you feel warmly welcomed and safe, and where the people are friendly and fun—and always happy to see you!

I love that Ruby Sawyer created a place like that for her foster kids, offering them a secure and loving home. Her farmhouse was a comforting refuge in a sharp-edged world, and it made a huge difference to six very wounded children. Even Nick, her adventure-loving foster son who grew up to visit so many beautiful places, still loved Ruby's simple house best of all.

From talking with my readers, I know that many of you, like Ruby, have created warm, comforting spaces for your family and friends. And of course, as we see in this story, it really doesn't matter if your home is large or small or fancy or simple. What really matters is the love and acceptance we offer to tired and hurting folks. What a sweet and much-needed ministry!

So, if you've created a cozy corner for someone who needed one, please consider yourself hugged. And I hope this story—and the others set in Cedar Ridge—will be a refuge for you, a sweet break from the busy world. You are always welcome here!

Much love,
Laurel

PS Let's stay in touch! You can sign up to become one of my "Front Porch Friends" by subscribing to my newsletter at laurelblountbooks.com! We have lots of fun every month, and I'd love to have you join us!